I ESCAPED THE SALEM WITCH TRIALS

JULIET FRY

SCOTT PETERS

I Escaped The Salem Witch Trials (I Escaped Book Six)

Library of Congress Control Number:

ISBN: 978-1-951019-18-1 (Hardcover)

ISBN: 978-1-951019-17-4 (Paperback)

Book cover design by Susan Wyshynski

Best Day Books For Young Readers

ONE

Salem, Massachusetts
Spring 1692

The air reeked of sweat and fear. In the front row of Salem's meetinghouse, five girls huddled together, shoulder-to-shoulder, knees pressed against knees.

One spoke in a frightened voice, too low for the crowd to hear.

"Louder," the judge ordered.

Her face shadowed beneath her wide-brimmed bonnet, the girl said, "A witch attacked me."

"How?" the judge asked.

"She sent her spirit to my house. She crushed me, and I couldn't breathe."

A murmur arose from the crowd.

Another girl spoke up. "A witch attacked me, too. She tried to make me sign the devil's book."

1

"Who are these witches?" the judge demanded. "Tell me."

One by one, the girls began to name names. They were villagers everyone knew: mothers and grandmothers, servants and relatives.

As the crowd listened, eleven-year-old Hannah sat next to her four friends in silence. She felt dizzy. She didn't belong on the accuser's bench. If the judge found out what she'd done, what she'd taken part in . . .

They said it was just a game.

The judge wouldn't see it that way.

The stuffy room grew hotter as guards hauled the accused women to the front. Some held their heads high; others were limp with terror.

Hannah wanted to get away.

Then, to her horror, the judge called on her.

"Hannah True," he asked, removing his spectacles to study her.

"Yes?"

"Did this accused woman standing before you hurt you?"

Hannah hesitated. "I . . . I don't know."

"You don't know?" the judge demanded.

Further down the bench, one of the girls stood. She pointed at Hannah. "She won't speak because she's one of them!"

Hannah gasped. "That's not true."

"Yes it is. You're a witch!"

Judge Hathorne said, "Hannah True, did you send your spirit to hurt these girls beside you?"

"No, of course I didn't!" Hannah reached for Ann's hand—Ann, who had always stood up for her. "You know this isn't true. Say something!"

Ann hesitated.

"I'm innocent," Hannah cried.

Ann wouldn't do this to her, would she? Everyone knew what happened to witches. If they arrested her, she'd be taken to jail.

She'd be on trial for her life.

How would she ever escape?

TWO

MONTHS EARLIER

Lightning scratched the night sky and thunder shook the windowpanes. Trees groaned, their powerful branches clawing at the little farmhouse.

Hannah curled herself into a ball, hugging her knees to her chest. Ratter paced next to her bed, panting hard. She reached out and touched the dog's fur, glad of his presence.

Beside her, the girl who shared her servant's duties in the Putnam house dozed on, oblivious. How could she sleep through this storm?

Bang!

Hannah jumped. What was that?

Bang, bang, bang!

The sound came from outside the window.

"Mercy," Hannah whispered, shaking her.

"What is it?" Mercy groaned sleepily.

"Someone's banging at the window!"

Thunder exploded and Mercy bolted upright. They both stared at the dark pane of glass. Outside, trees moaned in the howling storm.

"It's just the wind," Mercy finally said. "Go to sleep, the mistress's children will be awake early."

The Putnam's littlest ones always woke at the crack of dawn, and the girls were expected to keep them quiet so as not to wake the baby. But Hannah was too frightened to sleep.

She whispered a prayer: "Now I lay me down to sleep, I pray the Lord my soul to keep. If I should die before I wake, I pray the Lord my soul to take."

Lightning flashed; the split-second glare revealed long, skinny fingers clawing at the window.

"A witch!" Hannah cried.

"Where?"

"Outside, she's outside—she's trying to break the glass!"

Ratter ran in circles, barking and whimpering. Wide-eyed, the two servant girls stared at the now dark window.

They blinked as a silver moon blazed into view between two thunderclouds.

Then, dark silhouettes flew across the sky.

"Witches!" Hannah cried. "Did you see them?"

Before Mercy could reply, a shrieking gust was followed by what sounded like a heavy weight smashing down near the house.

Mercy screamed and Ratter barked.

"Quiet!' a deep voice roared. The door to their room flew open and a tall shape loomed on the threshold.

The figure raised a flickering candle. It was Mr. Putnam, their master, standing in his cap and nightdress.

"Ratter, bad dog!" he said. "And you girls, that's enough. It's just a storm."

The wind rose to fever pitch.

Hannah spoke up, her voice trembling. "There was a witch, at the window."

Mr. Putnam snorted. "A witch? Ridiculous. No witch would dare bother our family, Hannah True. They know we love the Lord, and that he protects us from evil."

Mercy said, "I know that, Mr. Putnam. Hannah was being silly."

Hannah stared at her shaking hands, feeling the weight of her master's glare.

"Go to sleep." Mr. Putnam blew out the candle and closed the door firmly.

"Someone was out there," Hannah whispered stubbornly.

"Go to sleep, or you'll get us both in trouble."

THREE

The morning dawned so cold that Hannah could see her breath. In the icy silence, her nighttime fears seemed ridiculous. She groaned. Had she honestly awoken Mr. Putnam with her screams?

"Mercy, wake up. We have to check on the children."

"You do it." Mercy rolled over, her masses of tangled red hair disappearing beneath the covers.

Something fluttered beyond the window's diamond-shaped panes. *Skinny fingers were pressed against the glass!*

But then a laugh escaped her.

Fingers? No, they were broken branches.

Shivering, she dressed quickly, pulling on thick stockings, scuffed shoes, and tucking her dark ringlets under a warm cap. Then she tiptoed to the washbasin. The water had frozen over.

Mercy called to her from under the covers. "It's your

turn to empty the chamber pot." She wrinkled up her nose, pointing to where they kept it under the bed. "It stinks something awful."

It wasn't Hannah's turn, but at seventeen, Mercy was a lot older and not always kind. She'd been with the Putnam family for ages, long before Hannah showed up. She was still sore at Hannah for cutting in on what she claimed was *her territory*. There was no point in arguing—Mercy would always find some way to make her life miserable.

Hannah donned her cloak and went outside to empty it in the privy.

"Good Morrow!" called Isaac, the Irish servant boy. Thirteen years old, he stood in the yard with a huge ax slung over one shoulder.

"Oh! Isaac." She gripped the full, foul-smelling chamber pot, wishing for the power to make it disappear.

Isaac smiled, his cheeks splotched pink from the cold. "Consider yourself lucky."

"Lucky?" Hannah edged toward the privy.

"A tree almost took out your room."

When she saw the fallen tree peeking out from the back of the house, she nearly stumbled. Another few feet and she and Mercy would have been crushed.

"Thank the Lord," Hannah whispered.

"I'm glad you're safe," Isaac said, his blue eyes earnest. "The branches just grazed your window."

"I thought they were witch's fingers," Hannah confessed, laughing.

"They do rather look like skinny fingers. But don't worry. I'll chop the witch's arm right off!"

Overhead, fluffy white clouds floated in the vast blue

sky. Birds twittered, and a pair of squirrels raced across the grass.

Isaac grinned and hefted the ax, swinging it in a wide arc.

But as it came down, it bounced off a knot in the wood, slipped to the side and, with a sickening thud, landed on his foot. He cried out and fell.

"Isaac!" Hannah gasped as blood bloomed across his boot. She fisted her hands, trying to keep her head from spinning, wanting to scream for her mother. But that wasn't possible.

"Breathe, take a deep breath," Hannah told him. "I need to stop the blood."

She tore a strip from her apron. Trying not to retch, she slowly edged the boot free. Blood gushed from the wound.

"My foot," he groaned.

Quickly, Hannah wrapped it tightly with the

makeshift bandage. "I need more bandages. And I have a salve my mother taught me to make. Stay here."

She ran inside and returned to find Isaac's bandage soaked crimson.

"Will I be all right?" he asked as she bound it up.

"When the bleeding slows, use this salve to stop any infection. You need to rest. Can you make it back to your cabin?"

He nodded.

She found him a branch for a crutch. "I promise I'll come check the wound later."

As he hobbled away, she was reminded of her gentle mother's healing hands and a big lump caught in her throat.

Her mother had been the village healer. She'd been able to cure almost anyone—except herself. When the fever came, Hannah's parents fell ill with shocking speed. Hannah had tried to save them using everything her mother taught her. But she'd failed them both. The pox outbreak stole them away.

Gulping hard, she held back stinging tears.

Isaac turned. "Thank you for helping me, Hannah," he called. "You're a fine healer."

Then why were her parents gone?

"Hannah?" Mercy called. "The baby's crying. What are you doing out there?"

Hannah emptied the chamber pot and hurried inside.

"What kept you?" Mercy demanded, smirking. "Were you chatting with the blacksmith's son again?"

Hannah scowled. She hated it when Mercy teased her.

Seated near the fire was the Putnam's eldest daughter,

Ann. She was twelve, only a year older than Hannah, yet she already seemed like an adult—maybe because she had four younger brothers and sisters. She held her littlest brother, baby Timothy, and glanced up, her blond hair framing her heart-shaped face.

"What happened to your apron?" she cried, aghast.

It was torn, dirty, and streaked with Isaac's blood.

"Isaac had an accident chopping wood. I used it to make a bandage."

"You used your good apron?" Mercy looked scornful. "Don't you know you won't get another?"

Hannah's face went hot. "It was an emergency."

"Well, you're going to look pretty stupid wearing that now," Mercy said, laughing. "People will think you're—"

"Mercy," Ann said. "Would you go up and help Mother with the children?"

With her back to Ann, Mercy's face darkened in a way that only Hannah could see. The older girl didn't like to be cut off.

"And Hannah," Ann said. "Mother needs you to run an errand over to the Parris's. Little Betty Parris has a stomachache. You're to bring them that mint tonic you made. Will you be alright walking alone?"

"Of course." Hannah felt a rush of gratitude toward Ann, who always came to her rescue whenever Mercy teased her. "I'll go right now."

Hannah fetched the tonic and hurried outside.

FOUR

The walk to the parsonage where the Parris family lived was a long one. The bitter wind sent leaves skittering across the dirt road.

She passed the meetinghouse where, twice a week, Reverend Parris gave his sermons. Hannah knew it was wicked to think it, but she often wished she didn't have to go. The Reverend always droned on for hours, the benches were hard, and these days it was so cold the bread froze to the communion plate!

A worn dirt laneway led to the parsonage.

Two dark-skinned servants worked away outside. The man, John Indian, was chopping wood, his blade slicing in great whacks. Tituba, his wife, carried the logs to the pile. She looked up, fixing her eyes on Hannah.

Hannah glanced away. Tituba's intense stares were unnerving.

She was glad to reach the front door.

Hannah's friend, Abigail threw it open, clearly flustered. Like Hannah, Abigail was an orphan, but she was lucky because her relatives had taken her in. Reverend Parris was her uncle, and the children were her cousins.

"I'm so glad you're here!" Abigail cried.

"I brought some tonic for Betty." Hannah held up the bottle in her half-frozen fingers. "It's my mother's recipe. I made it myself."

"Betty's in bed. Come on."

Upstairs, the Reverend kept an office where he wrote his lengthy sermons. Hannah took care to tiptoe past his door.

In the bedroom, little Betty huddled beneath the quilts, but she grinned when she saw Hannah.

"I hear you have a stomachache. This should make you feel better," Hannah said.

Abigail said, "Hurry up and take it, then get dressed. There's something we need to do."

Downstairs, Tituba was sweeping the floor. "Where are you girls going?"

"Oh, nowhere." Abigail shot Hannah a small, secret smile and led them toward the front door.

Hannah wondered what mischief she was up to.

Outside, they wound past the barn, through a stand of trees, down to the saltbox hut where Tituba and John Indian lived. Hannah looked nervously over her shoulder while Abigail peered through a gap in the hut's wall.

"We have to be fast." Abigail tried the door. It was unlocked.

"That's their house," Betty said. "We can't go in there. What if they catch us?"

"They're busy working."

John Indian could still be heard chopping wood.

"Hurry!" Abigail cried. "Come inside!"

The room smelled funny. It was cold, cramped, and gloomy.

Abigail whispered, "Do you believe in witches?"

Betty's eyes turned big and solemn. Hannah shivered, recalling last night's storm and how she'd screamed, sure that a witch was trying to break through the window.

"Of course I do," Hannah said. "It's a sin not to believe."

Her friend frowned. "I know that! But do you believe we have witches in *our village?*"

Hairs prickled on Hannah's arms. "I don't know. Let's get out of here. I don't want to get caught."

"They say witches use poppets to hurt their enemies." Abigail crossed to a rickety table beside Tituba's bed.

To Hannah's shock, Abigail picked up a small box and opened it.

Hannah stood glued to the spot. They shouldn't be looking in Tituba's things. Part of her wanted to run. Another part longed to know what the box contained.

Her friend lifted a dirty piece of linen. Underneath lay a crudely made doll.

Abigail gasped. "It's just like Mercy said. Tituba has a poppet."

Betty whimpered. "What's a poppet?"

Abigail's round eyes met Hannah's. "Can you believe she has this?"

"What's a poppet?" Betty said again.

"It's a doll that witches make, like a puppet of someone they hate. Then they jab needles into it, and it hurts the person."

Hannah said, "How did Mercy know it was here?"

"I don't know. She just said to look in Tituba's hut."

"I wanna go," Betty wailed.

"Put it away." Hannah took Betty's cold hand in hers. "You're scaring Betty!" In truth, it was scaring her, too.

"Don't you see?" Abigail said. "Tituba's a witch, and this is proof."

"It's just a doll. Tituba can't be a witch." Still, Hannah couldn't help recalling the woman's unsettling stare. "Mr. Putnam told me witches wouldn't dare bother our village because we love the Lord, and the Lord takes care of us."

"I thought you said it was a sin not to believe in witches," Abigail replied.

"I do believe!"

"If there are no witches in Salem," Abigail said carefully, "Then why did your parents die?"

Hannah flinched as if she'd been struck.

But Abigail went on. "And why did your mistress's baby die? And how did Constable Herrick's prize cow just vanish? Witches put curses on God's people. That's where the bad luck comes from."

Hannah fought to keep back tears. Could witches have cursed her parents? Maybe she wasn't to blame. She swallowed hard. "I don't know why my parents got sick. Or why the cows vanished. But I do know that babies die all the time."

"Think about it, Hannah," Abigail whispered, fingering the poppet. "Your mistress's baby died in a terrible way. It wasn't normal."

Betty's hand tightened around Hannah's.

Abigail went on. "You know exactly what I'm talking about. That little baby had awful fits, like . . . like someone was sticking needles into her. It's our duty to stop evil from hurting people. Don't you think?"

Outside, the noise of chopping wood stopped.

Abigail stuffed the poppet into the box, crammed the lid back on, and dropped it on the table.

"Quick!" she cried. "Let's get out of here."

FIVE

Hannah ran toward home, disturbed by the creepy poppet she'd seen in Tituba's hut. Was it really an evil witch's tool? Or was it just a simple doll?

The setting sun glowed orange through the bare trees and sent long shadows twisting across the road. She pulled her cloak tight against the icy wind.

The woods grew deeper, with row upon row of grey trunks crowding both sides of the dirt lane. A strange silence lingered, broken only by the occasional rustle of leaves.

Out of the corner of her eye, she saw something move among the shadowy rows. Hannah stopped dead, her heart slamming as she squinted into the gloom.

Something was in there. Goosebumps rose on her neck.

She resumed walking, faster now, and saw a flash of

movement. Maybe it was a deer. Or the wind. Or maybe . . . maybe, she was being followed.

She gathered up her skirts and ran. Through the barren branches, a beast with grey fur appeared not fifty paces away. Its yellow eyes gleamed in the shadows.

"*A wolf!*" she whispered.

Wolves never came this close to the village. But everyone knew witches could take on the shape of a wolf or any other animal. Was an evil witch following her?

The woods became a blur as her footsteps pounded on the road. All she could hear was her ragged breath. She clutched at the stitch in her side, frantic, and finally reached the farm's edge.

When she looked back, the road was empty. The wolf was gone.

Fingers shaking, Hannah unlatched the gate.

In the farmhouse, the roaring fire warmed the main room and her shoulders finally relaxed.

"Are you sure you saw a wolf?" Ann asked when Hannah told her what had happened. "I've never heard of a wolf in Salem Village."

"It was following me."

Mistress Putnam came downstairs, alarmed. "A wolf? You're certain?"

Ann put her arms around Hannah and hugged her. "I'm glad you're safe."

Mercy sneered. "I doubt it was a wolf."

Before Hannah could protest, a rap sounded at the front door. Ratter charged toward it, barking.

"Who could that be?" Mistress Putnam opened it, and a cold gust blew inside.

Sarah Good, the village beggar, stood there in ragged clothes with dirt streaking her face. Her little daughter stood next to her, clutching her mother's soiled apron.

"Good Morrow!" Sarah Good cried. "Mind if my child and I come in out of the cold?"

Mistress Putnam stepped back to allow them to enter, but her mouth formed a long, thin line.

Sarah rubbed her hands appreciatively, glancing around the cozy home. "It's so warm in here."

Hannah suddenly felt glad for her bed, even if she did have to share it with Mercy. She'd come to love this house; it was finally starting to feel like home.

"Warm yourself, and then go, please." Mistress

Putnam picked up Timothy, for the baby had started to whine.

"Is he sick?" Sarah stretched a filthy hand toward the child.

Her nails were dirty and cracked. Before Mistress Putnam could stop her, the beggar's grimy fingers touched the baby's cheek, and she whispered something inaudible.

Mistress Putnam jerked him away. "W—what did you say?"

"Oh, just a little prayer for the baby's health." Sarah Good smiled a crooked smile, revealing a missing front tooth.

A strange foreboding sent shivers down Hannah's spine.

"Hannah," Mistress Putnam said, her voice verging on panic. "Bring them the basket of apples from the kitchen. Quick now."

Hannah scurried away and returned with the shiny red fruit.

Sarah Good grinned. "Oh, thank you kindly. May the Lord bless you and your family. Now, you wouldn't have any beer, would you? I have a terrible thirst."

"No!" Mistress Putnam opened the door. "I must ask you to leave."

Sarah Good clung to her daughter's grubby hand. "But we've no place to go."

"Please, leave."

Sarah's eyes flashed a warning, and her gaze went again to the baby in Mistress Putnam's arms. "I hope for your sakes you people never find yourselves in need of charity." Lowering her voice, she again muttered under her breath. This time it sounded nothing like a prayer.

Mercy slammed the door.

"She cursed my baby!" Mistress Putnam whispered, her fingers covering Timothy's cheek where Sarah Good had touched him.

"Old witch," Mercy cried.

Hannah felt cold all over. She'd always thought Sarah Good was a harmless beggar. Now, she wasn't so sure.

An hour later, Hannah excused herself to the privy.

Outside, however, she turned in the opposite direction and headed toward Isaac's cabin. It was the first chance she'd gotten to check on his foot, and she hoped he was all right.

Isaac would surely have something to say about the poppet, the wolf, and Sarah Good. He was levelheaded. Maybe he could make sense of it all. She was looking forward to seeing him.

But when she got there, she found Isaac's cabin empty. At least it meant he must be feeling better. She turned away, disappointed to have missed him.

That night Hannah tossed and turned, while upstairs, baby Timothy wailed.

Mercy lit the candle. "Hannah, are you awake?"

"How could anyone sleep through all this?"

"Move. I'm getting up to see if Mistress Putnam needs help."

Hannah threw back the covers. "I could rub my mother's calming ointment on him, it's worked before."

Mercy sneered. "Ointment won't help get rid of Sarah Good's curse."

Needing to feel useful, Hannah lit the kitchen fire. She boiled water and steeped herbs she'd dried that summer the way her mother taught her—feverfew and valerian. She carried the calming tea up to Mistress Putnam's room.

"Mistress, here, drink this." She set it next to the bed. "Let me take Timothy downstairs. I can try my mother's soothing ointment on him."

Mercy raised an eyebrow. "I hope it's not that vile-smelling green stuff you made?"

Mistress Putnam interrupted. "Oh Hannah, you're as kind as your mother Lydia was. I'm sure you will be a fine healer one day."

Hannah flushed.

Downstairs, she laid Timothy on a cloth, removed his

clout, and looked for a rash. Just as she suspected—even in the dim candlelight, she could see angry red skin. She applied ointment and put on a fresh clout, whispering the soothing songs her mother had always sung to her. Finally, his eyes drooped shut.

Hannah rocked him by the fire as he slept. All he'd needed was some treatment for his rash.

Yet as the flames dwindled, she remembered the wolf on the road. She thought of Tituba's poppet, and of Sarah Good's strange, fierce whispers. An awful tension seemed to be building in the little village of Salem.

SIX

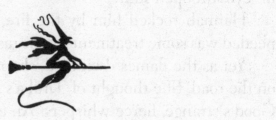

At dawn, Mistress Putnam granted the girls the morning off.

"We could go work on our quilting," Mercy said sweetly, winking at Ann.

Ann pulled a bonnet over her blond hair. "Good idea. Let's go."

On the road, Mercy linked a possessive arm through Ann's. Trees creaked in the wind, and a black crow flew in circles overhead.

Ann turned to Hannah and said, "Mercy has a new game to show us."

"You do? What is it?" Hannah said, happy for the distraction. While Mercy was often overbearing, she was never boring.

"You'll see," Mercy sang.

They quickened their pace, leaping over puddles and laughing. With her friends at her side, Hannah forgot all about witches and wolves until they reached the parsonage. But her fears came rushing back when Tituba answered the door.

"Good morrow, girls," Tituba said, staring at Hannah.

"We're here to work on the quilt," Mercy said.

"Enter, then." Tituba moved just enough for the girls to brush past. She smelled of wood smoke and sweat, reminding Hannah of the damp shack where they'd found the poppet.

Abigail jumped up to greet them. "Quilting time?" Her eyes twinkled. "Sit down and I'll fetch it."

As they sat around the fire, Hannah caught snatches of words about the poppet and said, "Does Tituba know you found it?"

"Shhhhh!!" Abigail's blue eyes flashed. "She's just in the kitchen. She'll hear you, you dolt!"

Hannah looked away, her cheeks hot.

Mercy pouted. "This is boring. Come on, I want to show everyone my game."

Abigail gave Mercy an impish smile. "What's the game?"

"It's a game that tells the future," Mercy said.

Betty's eyes widened; Ann and Abigail exchanged glances; Hannah's heart skipped. Fortune telling was a grievous sin. What if someone caught them?

'We must be quick," Abigail said, her eyes flicking toward the stairs. "How do we do it?"

"I need a glass of water and an egg."

In the kitchen, Mercy tossed her fiery hair, took an egg from the basket, and broke it, separating the yolk. She poured the egg white into a glass of water. "The shape it makes will tell us something about what our future holds."

"I bet I know what shape it's going to make for you, Mercy," Abigail said.

Both girls giggled, and Hannah wondered what they meant.

Ann, who'd been silently watching, pointed excitedly, "Look! It looks like a boat!"

Betty piped up. "Perhaps Mercy will travel to a distant land!"

Abigail smirked. "Or perhaps she'll marry a ship-builder like Nathaniel Ingalls of Salem Town!"

Mercy and Abigail tried to hold back their giggles. Ann, looking less certain, smiled, too.

"Shhh!" said Betty. "Someone will hear you. We shouldn't do this anymore. It's what witches do."

"She's right," Hannah whispered, genuinely concerned. "What if the Reverend catches us?"

"It's just a game," Mercy said and smirked. "Let's see what Hannah's fortune will be."

"I think we should stop," Hannah said.

Tituba could reappear, or the Reverend. Besides, Mercy would probably try to tease her about her friend, Isaac, again.

Mercy cracked an egg into the water. "Look! It's an anvil!" She laughed, hard.

Hannah saw no anvil but knew what Mercy was up to. Every blacksmith owned one and Isaac's father was teaching him to be a blacksmith. Mercy elbowed her, still laughing.

Ann seemed to sense Hannah was upset, for she took an egg and said, "Let's find out what my future will be."

Ann's egg white swirled and settled into a long, thin box-like shape that narrowed at the top. She stopped smiling.

"It's a coffin," Betty cried.

"No," Hannah said, peering harder. But it looked exactly like a coffin.

"Yes it is!" Betty whimpered.

Silently, Tituba appeared in the doorway. Abigail grabbed the glass and hid it behind her back.

"What are you girls doing?" Tituba asked.

Betty ran and buried her face in Tituba's apron, sobbing. The servant wrapped her arms around Betty's small form. "What have you done to scare her?"

"She's always scared," Abigail said. "We were just playing a game. But you better not snitch or we'll tell Reverend Parris about your *poppet*."

Hannah's mouth fell open—she'd never heard her friend talk this way.

Tituba frowned. "I don't have a poppet."

"Yes, you do," Abigail said. "We saw it. We all saw it."

"I don't know what you mean. Your talk is disturbing the child."

"Then let's talk no more," Abigail said.

Tituba scowled and left.

When they were alone again, Betty let out a muffled sob.

Mercy pointed at her. "If you tattle-tale, you'll be sorry!"

Hannah wondered what she and her friends had gotten themselves into.

SEVEN

"What did you girls do to upset Betty Parish so?" Mistress Putnam asked the next day.

"What do you mean?" Mercy replied, looking uneasy.

Ann colored slightly. Hannah stared at her hands. If anyone found out about their fortune-telling game . . . people might accuse them of practicing witchcraft, and well . . . all of Salem knew what happened to witches.

She should have stopped it.

Ann said, "We were just quilting."

Mistress Putnam frowned. "I got a message from the parsonage this morning wanting to know what happened yesterday. Betty is shaking and crying and saying things that don't make sense. No one knows what ails her."

Guilt washed over Hannah. "Let me take her a tonic to calm her nerves."

Mistress Putnam squeezed her arm fondly. "That

would be kind, Hannah. In fact, let's all go. I think it would be wise to pay the Parris's a visit together."

The girls shared an alarmed glance. What if Betty told on them?

"Ann, please fetch some soup for us to take," Mistress Putnam said. "We can lay hands on the girl and pray the Lord will heal her."

Ann nodded. "Of course, mother."

Mercy piped up, all innocence. "I'd better stay behind, Mistress. Someone needs to take care of the little ones."

"Yes, fine. Thank you, Mercy."

Ann and Hannah shot her a look. Mercy merely shrugged and smiled slyly from beneath her mop of red curls.

When Hannah, Ann, and Mistress Putnam arrived at the parsonage, they found a group of women already praying in the main room. The women's loud, fervent prayers couldn't drown out a strange sound, though. It was almost like a barking dog.

Hannah turned to Ann. "What's that noise? The Parris's don't have a dog."

"I think it's Betty," Mistress Putnam said, looking alarmed. She pushed through the group, and Hannah followed.

Betty's mother stood in the far corner, wringing her hands. "I don't know what's wrong with my little girl."

Hannah could hear groans and barks but couldn't see Betty anywhere. "Where is she?"

"In the cupboard," Betty's mother said. "She won't come out."

Hannah knelt and tried to coax Betty out. "What's wrong? Talk to me!"

But the child's screams only grew louder. Red-cheeked, her golden hair pasted to her damp forehead, Betty's face twisted in agony.

Hannah backed away, searching for Abigail. She would know what had happened.

Grey light filtered through the window where Abigail stood looking out. Hannah rushed to her friend's side with Ann on her heels.

"What happened after we left?" Hannah and Ann whispered.

But Abigail said nothing; she stared outside as if in a trance.

"Abigail?"

Silence. She didn't even turn. Instead, like a sleep-walker, she seemed unaware of her surroundings.

Hannah's heart thumped off beat. What was going on?

Mistress Putnam approached. "Hannah, where's the medicine you brought?"

Hannah's fingers went to her pocket where she'd placed her mother's tonic. It was ginger and chamomile, suitable for the vapors, but she had no clue what ailed Betty and Abigail. She'd never seen anything like it.

The front door opened, and the prayer circle abruptly stopped praying. The women moved aside as Reverend Parris and Doctor Griggs entered.

Reverend Parris said, "Thank you, ladies. Please return home, and pray that the Lord has mercy on our Betty."

As the women filed out, Hannah's mistress approached the doctor.

"Doctor Griggs," Mistress Putnam said. "This is Hannah True, the healer's daughter. She's made a tonic for Betty."

"The healer's daughter?" He studied Hannah with suspicion.

Hannah said, "It's to soothe the nerves."

At that moment, Abigail shrieked. She pushed away from the window, twisting and turning, arms flailing, body contorting at strange angles. The girl fell to the floor and her feet hammered the boards in a jolting, rhythmic clatter.

Hannah dropped the bottle in shock.

"Abigail!" Mistress Parris crouched over her niece. "What is it, my child?"

Peeling her lips back, Abigail snarled and snapped her teeth like a mad dog. Her aunt jerked away. Drool slid down Abigail's chin, and her eyes rolled in their sockets.

"This is no place for visitors," the Reverend said. "Mistress Putnam, take your girls and go. There is illness in this house."

Hannah picked up the medicine bottle and offered it to Dr. Griggs.

Dr. Griggs snorted. "Your healer's brew has no use here. Only prayer and fasting can help now. These girls have been cursed by witchcraft."

"Witchcraft?" Hannah stepped back in shock.

"Leave us," the Reverend said.

Terrified, Hannah hurried out the parsonage door, running to catch up with the others. She spied Tituba's shack and was struck with a pang of fear. What if Tituba was using her poppet to hurt Abigail? But Tituba loved Betty, so why was Betty sick?

What if this was because of Mercy's fortune-telling game? Had they brought this evil on themselves by experimenting with dark forces they couldn't control?

She reached Ann's side, and Ann linked one trembling arm through hers.

Mistress Putnam wore a dark look. "Mark my words, Sarah Good is behind this."

In all the chaos, Hannah had forgotten about the beggar-woman's disturbing visit. Could Sarah Good be responsible? She hated to think it, but wouldn't that be better than believing she and her friends were to blame for this horror? Was Sarah Good a witch?

Back home, Timothy's face was scarlet from crying. Mistress Putnam bundled him in her arms, rocking him and praying.

A frightening hour passed. Then, a village boy arrived with a message from the Reverend.

Mr. Putnam unfolded the note and began to read aloud. *"I caution you to stay away from the parsonage. And I ask that you pray for the souls of my daughter and my niece. Dr. Griggs has confirmed they are cursed. The children have named the witches—"*

"Witches?" Ann cried.

Hannah said, "They named more than one?"

"Who are they?" Mercy demanded.

Mr. Putnam folded up the letter. "Tituba, their slave." He glanced at his wife and crying son. "And I'm afraid the other witch is Sarah Good."

"Dear God." A damp sheen appeared on Mistress Putnam's forehead.

"They must be arrested immediately!" Mr. Putnam roared. "I'm going for Constable Herrick." He hurried outside.

Ann signaled Hannah and Mercy to follow her upstairs. In the bedroom, she closed the door. "Do you think Betty will tell the constable about the game?"

The three girls stared at one another. Hannah's stomach churned. If she did, would they be named as witches, too?

"Maybe we should tell my mother," Ann said.

"How would that help anyone?" Mercy said. "Do you want them to come for us? Besides, we didn't make Betty and Abigail sick. It was Tituba and Sarah Good."

Oh, if only Hannah's mother were still alive! What would she say? She'd know what to do. Hannah could tell her anything.

The question brought her crashing down to earth. There were lots of reasons a person got sick. And most had nothing to do with witchcraft.

Hannah blurted, "We should be careful what we say. Mercy's right."

Mercy was taken aback but then nodded. "Thank you, Hannah."

Ann said, "I'm afraid."

"We'll be fine. We just need to stick together," Hannah said.

Ann nodded. "All right."

All three held hands and agreed.

EIGHT

That evening, Timothy seemed calmer. The whole family settled down in the main room after dinner. The logs crackled and the warmth felt good. One could almost imagine that the awful illness afflicting their friends was nothing more than a strange dream.

Hannah was tending to the fire when Ratter started to bark.

"Is someone outside?" Ann said.

"It's the wind," her mother said.

Hannah rose and opened the door. A cold gust sent leaves tumbling through. "No one's there."

Shutting it, she turned to see Ratter's fur standing on end. The dog's soft brown eyes were fastened on Mercy. Something strange was happening; Mercy was doubled over as if in agony.

Ratter growled at her, long and low.

"Mercy?" Mistress Putnam cried.

The girl clutched her stomach and moaned.

"Mercy!" Hannah ran to her, but the girl recoiled from Hannah's touch.

Meanwhile, Ann's eyes had gone eerily blank. Her right arm began to twitch and she shouted over Ratter's shrill barking. "No, no, don't hurt me!"

"Ann, what is it?" Mistress Putnam cried. "What do you see? Who hurts you?"

But Ann thrust out her arms as though pushing away an invisible attacker. "No," she shouted. "I won't do it!"

"What is all this?" Mr. Putnam thundered. "What won't you do?"

Ratter barked louder, Timothy howled, and Mercy began a high-pitched keening wail that rattled Hannah to her core. What was happening?

"Please!" Ann screamed, "Please, don't make me!"

Mr. Putnam took hold of his daughter's shoulders. "Child! Who do you see?"

Ann just stared past him. He shook her, hard.

"No, don't!" Mistress Putnam cried, flying at him.

All of a sudden, the candles flickered and a hard gust sent the door flying open. The wind extinguished the flames, plunging the room into shadows. Hannah ran and slammed it shut.

The cold seemed to wake Ann from her trance. Her face was lit only by the red glow of the smoldering fire.

"It was Sarah Good," she whispered. "Papa, she had the devil's book and she wanted me to sign it."

"The devil's book?" His voice grew dark with rage.

"I refused, Papa. I refused."

Mistress Putnam leaped to her feet, frantic. "Thomas, you must stop that witch!"

"Oh, I will stop her," Mr. Putnam said.

Before he could explain what he meant to do, Mercy began to writhe across the floor, making strange inhuman sounds. Hannah stared, sick with fear. The shutters began to rattle wildly and rain pelted the house. It felt like an evil force was trying to get in.

Still convulsing on the floor, Mercy lashed out, sweeping a chair aside and sending it crashing into the wall. "No, Goody Osborne," she shouted. "No! I won't sign my name in that book. Why do you torment me? What have I ever done to you?"

Hannah could hardly believe her ears. *Goody Osborne?* Was Mercy seeing *another* witch? Goody Osborne was a sickly old woman who rarely left her bed. How could she send her spirit here?

Ann renewed her screaming. "She's pinching me! Oh, Papa! Stop her!"

"Who is pinching you?" Mr. Putnam shouted.

"Goody Osborne!"

"But how?" Hannah blurted. "She's old and sick and never leaves her bed."

Mr. Putnam said, "Goody Osborne is an evil woman. She has not set foot in church for almost three years."

"But—"

Mercy bolted upright and pointed to the fireplace. "I see a man, he's being roasted on a spit!" She moaned as though the image was too much to bear.

"Salem is being overrun by evil!" Mr. Putnam said.

Hannah sucked in a breath; the air smelled of spent candlewicks and wax.

Mercy thrashed wildly and ran toward the hearth. She lunged at the flames, clearly planning to jump into the fire. Just before her feet hit the grate, Mr. Putnam grabbed her. She screamed and twisted in his arms, strangely strong for a girl her size.

"Help me take her upstairs to the bedroom where she can't hurt herself," Mr. Putnam yelled.

Hannah ran to him as a clap of thunder shook the house. It was a fight to get Mercy under control. Ratter barked incessantly, weaving between their legs. They dragged her to the upstairs bedroom and secured the door from the outside.

Mr. Putnam turned to Hannah. Something in his gaze unnerved her. "I must ask you again, what were you girls up to yesterday?"

"N-nothing," she stammered. "We were sewing."

"Then answer me this. You're the only girl who's not afflicted. Why is that?"

"I—I don't know."

"Hmm."

Gurgling moans came from beyond the closed door. He was right. Why hadn't she fallen ill like the others?

"This stops tonight," Mr. Putnam said. "These witches must be rounded up to keep them from practicing their dark arts."

"But the storm . . ." Hannah replied.

"Do you seek to stop me?"

"Of course not!"

"Go downstairs."

"Yes, sir."

In the main room, Mr. Putnam whispered into his wife's ear. They both looked at Hannah. Then he pulled on his coat.

As he slammed outside, Mistress Putnam shot her a suspicious look. Hannah felt confused and frightened in a way she didn't dare voice. Not even to herself.

NINE

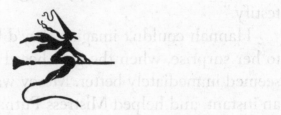

At dawn, Mr. Putnam came galloping back. He didn't bother to remove his muddy boots or sodden coat but instead strode straight to where his wife sat near the fire.

Hannah hung back, uncertain.

"Have the children's fits stopped?" he asked his wife.

"They have, Praise God."

He nodded briskly. "I told you I'd stop them, and I have. We've put the three witches in shackles so they can't practice their evil arts."

They'd put frail old Goody Osborne in shackles?

Uncertain of what to say, Hannah asked, "May I make you some breakfast?"

Mr. Putnam turned sharply, only now noticing her. "That won't be necessary," he said carefully. "You will help Mrs. Putnam and the girls get dressed. The trial is today, and we must stand witness."

"Today—already?" Hannah said.

"We must get to the root of this immediately. Wouldn't you agree?"

"Of—of course!"

"Then do as I say. My daughter and Mercy must testify."

Hannah couldn't imagine they'd be well enough. But to her surprise, when the girls heard about the trial, they seemed immediately better. Mercy was up and dressed in an instant, and helped Mistress Putnam with the younger children. Ann came downstairs dressed and ready to go, her cheeks flushed.

They all loaded into the wagon and rode for the meetinghouse. No one said much, yet Mercy and Ann's eyes were shining. Hannah offered to hold Timothy, but her mistress held him tight and turned away. Hannah swallowed hard. Were they upset with her?

At the meetinghouse, it looked like the whole village had come to see the witches' trial.

The crowd hummed with excitement.

Hannah's master turned to his wife and proudly said, "Justice Hathorne and Justice Corwin have come all the way from Salem Town to question the accused."

Despite sharing the name, Salem Town and Salem Village were miles apart. Hannah was surprised; important men such as Jonathan Corwin and John Hathorne only came to judge matters that affected the whole region.

How had they heard so quickly?

This whole business was growing out of control.

A nervous thrumming started in her stomach as the crowd parted to let them pass.

They strode to the reserved bench at the front. Reverend Parris and his wife were already there, sitting with two of their children. Hannah saw no sign of Betty and Abigail, though.

Were her friends still too sick to appear? She tried not to picture poor Betty barking in the cupboard.

Turning, she finally caught sight of Abigail, who sat in a hastily erected witness stand at the front.

"Go up and join her, girls," Mr. Putnam told Ann and Mercy. To Hannah, he said, "Not you. You're not afflicted."

Feeling awkward, Hannah sat gingerly alongside Mr. Putnam.

Meanwhile, up in the witness stand, her three friends huddled together, whispering amongst themselves. She nearly wished she was one of the afflicted, too. But that was nonsense.

The judges took their places at the pulpit. Justice

Hathorne with his long, grim face, and Justice Corwin with his scowl and balding head looked scary in their black robes.

"I call this trial to order!" Justice Hathorne said. "Constable Herrick, bring in the accused."

TEN

I n the meetinghouse, clothes rustled as everyone turned to see the prisoners.

The three accused witches were led to the front by a rope.

Tituba's eyes were wild with terror. Old, sickly Sarah Osborne stepped carefully along the aisle as if afraid she'd fall. But the beggar, Sarah Good, stuck out her chin, surveying the crowd with disbelief and resentment.

Sarah Good, was questioned first.

"Goodwife Good," Justice Hathorne thundered. "What evil spirits do you know?"

"None," she answered tartly, looking faintly disgusted.

"Have you had contact with the devil?"

"No"

"Why do you hurt these children?"

"I have ne—"

He cut her off. "What dark creatures are you using to spy on and hurt these poor innocents?"

Sarah Good snorted. "This is nonsense. I've done nothing wrong!"

"Silence!" The judge turned to address Hannah's friends. "Is this the woman that hurt you?"

To Hannah's dismay, the girls began to thrash and writhe in their seats.

"She pinched me this very morning," cried Ann, showing red welts on her arm. "Oh, it's happening again! She's hurting me. Make her stop!"

The crowd stared in horror as the girls cried and screamed, clearly in awful pain.

Justice Hathorne bellowed at Sarah Good. "Stop this madness, woman!"

"I'm just sitting here," Sarah Good replied.

"Why do you lie? It's clear you hurt these children! You continue to torment them." He gestured to the suffering girls.

"I do not," said Sarah Good stubbornly.

Mistress Putnam suddenly rose and pointed at her.

In a loud voice, she cried, "This woman came to my house begging, and while she was there, she muttered a curse. Ever since my baby has been ill."

"Sarah Good, what curse did you mutter at the Putnam's house?" the judge demanded. "What curse have you laid upon this infant?"

Sarah Good rolled her eyes. "I was only thanking the Putnam's for their charity! I have been falsely accused. I'm not a witch!"

"Well, who bewitched these children, then?"

"I don't know."

"Was it you?"

"No."

"Well then, who was it?"

Sarah Good sighed. "I said, I don't know."

"Who else in this village could be the witch then?"

"Maybe Sarah Osborne? You arrested her, also."

Sickly Sarah Osborne, who stood clinging to the rope around her wrists, glanced up; her mouth opened in shock.

"Sarah Osborne, come to the front," Judge Hathorne called.

Sarah Osborne was weak and frail but still tidy. Unlike Sarah Good's filthy rags, Sarah Osborne's clothes were simple but mended, and her hands were clean.

"Sarah Osborne, why do you torment these children?" the judge asked.

"I've never hurt any one of these girls."

"She's lying!" they shrieked, all starting to tremble violently and howl.

The sound was so horrible that Hannah clapped her hands over her ears.

"Why are you doing it now?" the judge shouted over the din.

"I'm not," Sarah Osborne insisted. "I don't know what ails them."

"Girls," roared the judge. "Please stand. Now tell me, is this woman before you the witch that has been tormenting you?"

"Yes!" Mercy cried, "She tried to strangle me!"

"She came to my house last night and poked me with knitting needles!" Ann said. "She was wearing exactly the same dress as she is now."

Hannah studied Sarah Osborne with fear. Could this frail woman truly possess that kind of power?

Stooped and thin, Sarah Osborne said, "I don't understand. I've never hurt them! I'm more likely to be bewitched myself than be a witch!"

"What do you mean by this?" the judge asked.

"I have horrible nightmares. An Indian comes into my room and pinches me, and drags me by my hair out the front door. Sometimes I hear voices calling my name."

"These voices—was that the devil speaking to you?" the judge thundered.

"I do not know the devil," she replied in a quiet voice.

"And yet you do not go to church."

"I have been very ill. I have kept to my sickbed. Everyone knows this."

The girls started to shriek, "Help, she's hurting me!"

Someone in the audience yelled, "Lock her up!"

Others joined the chorus. "Lock her up!"

"Constable Herrick, take these women to the Salem Town jail," Judge Hathorne instructed.

Hannah watched as the two women were dragged away. What would happen to them?

Next, Judge Hathorne called on Tituba, who nervously licked her lips.

"Why do you hurt these children?"

"I don't hurt them at all," Tituba stammered, looking confused.

"Who hurts them then?"

"The devil for all I know."

"Does the devil tell you he hurts them?"

"No, he tells me nothing."

"What does he look like when he hurts them?"

At this question, Tituba looked even more confused. Her eyes darted around the room. She paused as though scrambling for something to say.

"Well . . . he looks like a man, I think."

"A man from this village?"

The whole room grew hushed. Even the girls did not murmur.

"Yesterday, I was in my room," Tituba said, "And I saw a thing like a man, and he told me to serve him. And I told him, no, I would do no such thing."

Hannah stared. Could this be true?

"Have you seen anyone else with this devil?"

"Yes, at least nine people, I think."

The audience gasped.

"Can you name them?"

Tituba hesitated. Her face shone with sweat.

"If you know their names, you must tell us!"

Tituba swallowed. "Sarah Good and Sarah Osborne are two of them. I don't know the names of the others. Some tall man from Boston was with them. They told me to hurt the children, but I would not do it. I love little Betty."

"What else?" the judge pressed.

"They all hurt the children, but they put the blame on me. That's why these here girls are saying I'm a witch. But the man and those witches, they told me they'll hurt me worse than they ever hurt those girls because I wasn't gonna obey them."

"Did you ever hurt the girls?"

Tituba looked down. "Yes, but I will hurt them no more."

Tituba admitted it? So she was really a witch? Her power was real? If this was true, Hannah needed to tell the judge about the poppet. They needed to find it and burn it, or whatever you were supposed to do to destroy the evil thing.

But then Tituba began a dreadful tale of how the devil visited her in different forms—a raven, a black cat, a great black dog—and demanded she serve him. She said she saw him take a wolf's shape, and follow Lizzie Hubbard.

A wolf? Hannah gasped and found herself rising to her feet. In an unsteady voice, she cried, "That happened to me, too! A wolf followed me to the farm!"

Tituba nodded solemnly.

Hannah glanced toward Mercy, who'd laughed at her the day she'd run home scared. But Mercy was busy leaning on Ann's shoulder and moaning.

"Tituba, did you torment the Putnam children last night?" Judge Hathorne asked.

"They make me go. They flew me through the air and over the treetops to the Putnam's farm. Only Ann Putnam and Mercy, the serving girl, could see me. They ordered me to cut off Ann's head with a knife."

Next to Hannah, Mr. Putnam stood up. "It's exactly what Ann told me!"

"I would not do it!" Tituba cried. "I told them no, and they said they would cut my neck, but I would not do it!"

The girls began to scream and writhe.

Tituba's creepy confession was so disturbing that

JULIET FRY & SCOTT PETERS

Hannah wanted to get away. She heard the judge consign Tituba to prison with the others to await trial.

"Tituba saw nine witches?" Mistress Putnam whispered to her husband, loud enough for Hannah to hear. "How can there be nine more witches in our village? We must learn their names."

"Do not worry, we will." Mr. Putnam spoke with a clenched jaw, and glanced at Hannah. "I won't let them hurt my family."

A warning bell went off in her head.

Things were spiraling out of control. She had a sudden urge to run far away, to escape from Salem Village and never come back.

ELEVEN

T he next morning, Hannah stood in the yard, washing aprons, when Ann and her father returned home in their horse-drawn wagon.

"Another witch has been named!" Ann leaped down, her face lit with excitement. "It's Goodwife Nurse!"

Hannah inhaled sharply. "Goodwife Nurse? But she's so pious. She never misses church."

"She's a know-it-all." Ann tucked her fair hair behind her ears. "She's always telling everyone else what to do."

Hannah glanced toward the Nurse's farm, which lay next door. The Putnam and the Nurse families had been feuding over their shared boundary line for ages. Both were trying to claim ownership over the same piece of land.

Carefully, Hannah said, "Who named Rebecca Nurse as a witch?"

"I did!"

"Why?"

Ann pulled a face. "Why? Because last night while I was trying to sleep, she sent her spirit into my room to sit at the foot of my bed. She told me that if I didn't sign the devil's book, she'd choke me. I tried to scream, but my voice wouldn't work." Ann pulled aside her collar to reveal a dark bruise. "Look! I got this from her choking me."

"Oh! That's terrible, are you all right?" Hannah cried, shocked, for Ann did indeed have a bruise. She gave her a hug.

"I'll be all right when we get rid of these witches," Ann murmured.

After Ann went inside, Hannah got back to her washing. She didn't notice Isaac appear until he was standing before her. She jumped, startled.

"You seem ill at ease," Isaac observed.

"Oh! Isaac, I didn't see you. How is your foot? I tried to check on you earlier but you weren't there."

He grinned. "It's much better. Your salve worked. Now, what's going on?"

Hannah pushed her hair from her face with a soapy hand. "Ann's been attacked. Again. This time it was Rebecca Nurse."

Isaac raised an eyebrow. "And you believe this to be true?"

"She has bruises on her neck from being choked."

Isaac nodded slowly, but his eyes were filled with disbelief.

"It is hard to picture Goodwife Nurse as a witch," Hannah admitted. "She's always praying and doing good works in the village."

Isaac shoved his hands into the pockets of his canvas breeches. "Yesterday, Goodwife Nurse came to Mistress Putnam with some silly story that you girls were telling fortunes."

Fear whiplashed down Hannah's spine. How did Goodwife Nurse know?

Isaac shrugged. "Maybe that's why Ann's so eager to accuse her. For revenge. Anyway, I'm pretty sure everything Ann and Mercy say is a lie."

"I don't think they'd lie . . ." Hannah shifted uneasily, recalling their pact to keep their game a secret. How had Goodwife Nurse found out? Was she paying the price? Was Hannah somehow responsible?

"They like the attention," Isaac was saying.

Hannah's mind ran on. If Ann was lying to protect her and Mercy and the others, then why didn't she say so? They were friends. They were in this together.

But ever since Ann, Mercy, Abigail, and Betty had become afflicted, she'd begun to feel shut out.

The next day, Mr. Putnam told the girls to grab their cloaks while he pulled the wagon around. "A meeting is being held at Ingersoll's Tavern. I want you three girls there to testify."

"Why is Hannah coming?" Mercy glanced scornfully at Hannah. "She's not afflicted."

"Do as I say, and meet me out front."

As the girls pulled on bonnets and laced their boots,

Mercy eyed Hannah. "Did you hear about Lizzie Hubbard?"

Hannah frowned; Lizzie often joined their sewing group. "You mean about the wolf following her, like Tituba said at the trial?"

"No. Funny, Ann didn't tell you?"

Hannah turned to Ann, who laced up her boots and shrugged.

Mercy said, "Rebecca Nurse sent her spirit to attack Lizzie, too. Just like she attacked Ann. Actually, it was worse. They say the witch's spirit crawled inside Lizzie and tried to rip out her insides. And after, Lizzie was blinded for a nearly whole hour."

"But—" Hannah paused, checking herself. "How awful."

"Isn't it funny how you haven't been attacked?" Mercy said. "It *is* strange, isn't it, Ann? You have to wonder, what could Hannah be doing to protect herself?"

"I'm not doing anything," Hannah said.

Ann said, "Father's brought the wagon around. Let's go."

Hannah sat in silence as they rode into the village, while Ann and Mercy whispered together.

At Ingersoll's Tavern, Abigail and Lizzie Hubbard stood waiting for them outside the door. Hannah caught Abigail's eye and smiled, but the girl stared coldly and linked arms with Mercy. Was this because Hannah hadn't fallen ill?

It wasn't her fault.

The girls entered in a procession, heads held high, noses in the air. Hannah trailed after them.

She suddenly felt furious. At all of them. Even Ann. They didn't look like victims, but rather like they enjoyed the attention, just like Isaac had said.

Normally, Ingersoll's Tavern was a cozy place with a roaring fire, plenty of cider, and loud, friendly chatter. Today the mood was subdued.

The village leaders sat with the girls at a large table in one corner. Hannah was forced to find standing room against one wall. The leaders asked the girls questions and listened to their replies as though they were witch experts.

Hannah could only catch snatches of the conversation.

Nearby, a fat woman piped up. "Did you hear that? They've named some more witches! One of them is a man!"

"A man?" Hannah said. "Who?"

"The farmer, John Proctor, and his wife, Elizabeth!"

Hannah froze in place. Elizabeth Proctor? But she'd been her mother's dearest friend. Hannah still visited her often. Why would Mercy and the others do this? Not only was it impossible to picture Elizabeth Proctor practicing witchcraft, her husband, John Proctor, was a kind man and a highly respected member of the community.

Hannah was overcome with despair.

She felt dizzy and had to support herself against the wall as people began shouting, "Arrest the Proctors!"

Hannah saw Mercy and Lizzie standing in a corner, laughing. Her blood ran cold. How could they laugh?

Is that what they thought the witch-hunt was? An entertaining sport?

It was like they were consumed with their newfound power. People believed them, and they were growing reckless.

Who would they name next?

On the one hand, Hannah had seen witches attacking her friends with her own eyes. But she feared Mercy and the others were starting to make things up, to accuse innocent people.

She needed to speak out. But did she dare?

Who would believe her?

TWELVE

For long, dreary days, everyone prayed in the musty parsonage to God for guidance. But nothing seemed to help. Hannah felt weak from days of fasting, baby Timothy got no better, and the girls continued to have frightening fits that came and went.

"Hannah!"

She was peeling turnips and jumped at the sound of Mercy's voice.

"Let's go," Mercy called. "Ann and I want to talk to Abigail. It's important. We think you'd better come."

Reluctantly, Hannah set out alongside them.

On the road, the sun warmed Hannah's back and the fields bloomed with tiny white and yellow flowers. She even spied bluebells at the foot of a large tree. But they did nothing to banish her dark fears.

Mercy and Ann seemed oblivious, for they skipped ahead, laughing.

Half a mile from the parsonage, Abigail appeared, her fair hair backlit by the golden sun. Lizzie and a few other girls were with her.

"I'm glad you've come." Abigail spoke in a strange, singsong voice.

Something felt off about the way she talked. The sun no longer felt warm and the cool breeze had teeth. Hannah shivered.

Abigail led the way through the field, parting the flowers and long grass, and sat beneath a tall Beech tree.

Hannah followed, but every part of her wanted to turn and run away.

When they were arranged in a circle, Abigail spoke.

"I have some terrible news," she said. But her words contrasted strangely with the smile she wore. "I saw from the parsonage window a most dreadful sight."

Ann leaned forward, breathless. "What did you see?"

"The witches sought to mock us by holding their own communion supper in the pasture outside our holy parsonage."

Ann gasped.

"I was there, and I saw it, too!" Lizzie said, her eyes huge. "Forty witches or more, and they were having a ceremony. And instead of bread, they had red meat, and instead of wine, they drank blood!"

Hannah gaped. "Did the Reverend see them?"

Abigail's pale eyes went cold, like goat's eyes. "Of course not. He's not one of the afflicted. How could he see that? This is why we need to speak up. It's our solemn duty to name the witches."

Abigail wanted to accuse *forty people* of witchcraft? Hannah swallowed hard.

"Could you recognize any of them?" Mercy asked.

"I saw Elizabeth Proctor serving the supper."

Elizabeth Proctor, again?

"Others were wearing cloaks with hoods. But guess who the wizard in charge of everything was?"

"Who?" Hannah said.

"Reverend George Burroughs!"

"*Reverend*—but he used to be a village minister," Hannah cried, shocked.

Ann began nervously plucking at the grass. "His spirit came to me last night. He confessed that he murdered his first two wives." Her gaze met Hannah's.

The story sounded so stupid that Hannah snorted out loud.

Ann drew back, clearly wounded. "Are you laughing

at me? I was so scared. He was sitting right at the end of my bed! Don't you believe me?"

"No one would believe it, Ann! If he was a wizard, why would he tell you he killed his wives? He'd keep it a secret. It doesn't make sense!"

Mercy's eyes narrowed dangerously. "The village leaders trust us. Yet *you* seem to doubt our story. Do you think we're lying?"

"I never said that, it's just—"

Mercy sneered. "Here's what you need to understand. The Lord is using us to reveal the witches."

Hannah turned to Ann. "Are you honestly going to send forty villagers to jail? They'll be hung, you know. Hung until they're dead. These are people we've known all our lives."

Tears dampened Ann's lashes. "If you're not with us, then it seems you are against us." Her voice shook with emotion. "And why would that be so, when we are doing God's will?"

Seeing Ann's tears, Hannah backtracked. "I think you believe what you're saying, but . . ."

"Because it is true!" Ann said. "Tomorrow, we are to stand before the village elders to help question the new witches we've identified. Hannah, *please!* You must show your support for us!" Ann's eyes locked with hers, her expression earnest.

Hannah realized that her former friend was trying to help her.

Heart racing, she had no idea what to say.

THIRTEEN

The next morning, Ann took Hannah's hand as they rode in the wagon to the village. Once there, the crowd parted as though they were royalty.

The air inside Salem's meetinghouse smelled of sweat and fear. In the front row, the girls huddled together, shoulder-to-shoulder, knees pressed against knees—Hannah, Ann, Mercy, Abigail, and Lizzie Hubbard.

Lizzie Hubbard wore a glazed look. Ann's hands were fisted at her sides. Hannah shrank down in her seat.

Reverend Parris opened the meeting with prayer. Then he moved aside for Judge Hathorne, who got straight to the point.

"If there are witches in this town, I must know their names."

Ann spoke in a frightened voice, too low for the crowd to hear.

"Louder," the judge ordered.

Her face shadowed beneath her wide-brimmed bonnet, Ann said, "A witch attacked me."

"How?" the judge asked.

"She sent her spirit to my house. She crushed me, and I couldn't breathe."

A murmur arose.

"Guards! Bring the one of the accused to the front," Judge Hathorne commanded.

Hannah covered her mouth when she saw that it was her mother's best friend, Elizabeth Proctor.

A commotion sounded on a nearby bench. It was John Indian, Tituba's husband. He began drumming his feet up and down and shaking, his eyes rolling around in his head. Was he one of the afflicted, too?

Judge Hathorne said, "John Indian, who was it that hurt you?"

John Indian rocked faster in his seat. "It was Goodwife Proctor!"

"What did she do to you?"

"She brought me the devil's book."

Hannah stared, mortified. This had to stop.

Judge Hathorne's thick brows knit into a frown. "The devil's book? That is a grave accusation. Tell the truth, John Indian."

Hope stirred in Hannah's heart. The judge didn't believe him! Elizabeth Proctor would go free.

"It's true," John Indian moaned. "She comes to me and pinches me, and chokes me because I won't sign the devil's book."

"What do you say to these accusations, Goodwife Proctor?" Judge Hathorne asked.

"I know nothing of it," she cried. "I never hurt this man, God in heaven is my witness!"

The judge addressed the bench of the afflicted girls. "Ann Putnam, did this woman hurt you?"

"Yes sir, a great many times," Ann replied in a loud, clear voice.

Outrage filled Hannah.

But Ann's whole body began to tremble and the girls joined her, rocking and shaking in a horrible, frantic way that made the bench shudder.

"I never touched her!" Elizabeth Proctor cried. "Lying is a great sin against God, child."

Suddenly, Ann began twitching so hard she kept hitting Hannah in the arm. "Look! Goodwife Proctor's sent her spirit up onto the beam! Watch out!"

Nothing was up there. Yet Ann's face had gone white.

"Tell us what Goodwife Proctor is doing," the judge demanded.

Instead of answering, Ann began to choke and gurgle.

"It's a man—he's attacking her," Abigail cried. "It's Goodman Proctor, Goodwife Proctor's husband. He stops her mouth from speaking. He's an evil wizard!"

Goodman Proctor was the last person Hannah could ever picture as a wizard. With his honest eyes and skin sunburned from farm work, he'd always been kind. Hannah's outrage grew.

"Ann Putnam," Judge Hathorne said. "Who chokes you, child?"

"Goodman Proctor!" Ann screamed, thrashing her arms as though fending off invisible blows.

Hannah dug her nails into her palms, watching in

alarm as the Proctors were dragged from the building. She had to speak up for them. But say what?

The trial swept onward.

An older, well-dressed woman was led to the front. Clearly, she was not from Salem Village. She wore the finery only someone from the larger, bustling Salem Town could afford. Her sleeves were trimmed with silver lace and she wore a silk scarf. She held her head high, but her eyes shone with terror.

"Mistress English," Judge Hathorne said. "Did you send your spirit to hurt these girls before you? Did you hurt Ann Putnam and Abigail Williams?"

"I don't even know these girls. I've never laid eyes on them before." Her fingers nervously played with her scarf. Suddenly, it came loose and she fumbled with the brooch, re-pinning her scarf back together. As she did, Ann howled, causing Hannah to jump.

"Ann, what happened?" Hannah cried.

Her face contorted and she pointed at Mistress English. "She hurt me, ow! She hurt me!"

"Did you just prick Ann Putnam?" Judge Hathorne asked Mistress English.

A damp patch appeared on the woman's forehead. "I don't know," she stammered.

"Take the pin out," Judge Hathorne directed.

She nodded, pulling the pin from her scarf, her fingers trembling.

"Now put it back in again."

The girls all screamed in pain as Mistress English re-pinned the scarf.

"And again," the judge ordered.

Suddenly something sharp pierced Hannah's arm and she cried out. Pulling back her sleeve, she stared at the crimson bead of blood welling up. Her head spun. So it was all true? Everything her friends had said was true?

"Look!" Ann cried. "Mistress English attacked Hannah! Blood is running out from her wound!"

The crowd fell silent.

"Did Mistress English do this to you, Hannah?" Judge Hathorne asked.

The room got very hot.

Ann slid her hand into Hannah's and squeezed, hard.

Hannah hesitated. "I . . . I don't know."

"You don't know?" the judge demanded. "How did you come to be injured?"

Every afflicted girl studied her; Mercy and Lizzie Hubbard's eyes were like hot coals. Something about their expressions caused a wave of doubt.

A sharp object had indeed pricked her arm, but could it truly have been the scarf pin? If that woman was a witch, would she do something so stupid? Wouldn't she want to hide her guilt instead of pricking people with her scarf pin? It made no sense.

But what had jabbed her?

Ann was still holding her arm tightly.

Judge Hathorne cleared his throat. "You are injured," he repeated. "Did Mistress English do this to you?"

Hannah looked away. She remembered Ann's words—*you're with us or you're against us.*

Hannah could be safe. She could be one of them.

But she would have to accuse Mistress English. The woman would surely die and her death would be on Hannah's hands. Her mother had raised her to help people, not harm them.

"I don't know," she began. "I don't know for certain that it was her . . ."

But then something terrible happened. Ann's fingers brushed against Hannah's skirt and a second later, she pulled out a rusty nail.

"What's this?" Ann gasped, recoiling from Hannah. "Look! She has a nail. It was in her pocket! She pricked herself so that no one would suspect she's a witch!"

Hannah stared in dismay at her friend, who held the nail up for the judges to see.

"That's not mine!" Hannah said.

Further down the bench, Mercy stood and pointed at her. "She's one of them!"

Beside Mercy, Abigail tossed her blond hair from her face shouted, "Look! Up on that beam!" She pointed, her expression wild. "It's Hannah True's spirit. She's taken the form of a blackbird!"

"Hannah True!" Ann sobbed. "I can't believe you are one of them!"

Hannah reached for Ann's hand—Ann, who had always stood up for her. "You know this is a lie. Say something!"

Ann cast her eyes down and pulled away. She began to shudder and writhe, moaning and falling to the floor, her back arching, tears streaming down her face.

Hannah's throat constricted at the betrayal. "No. Please."

But Ann shouted, "All this time, you pretended to be a

healer. You were hurting people! Now I know why my baby brother is so ill!"

"I would never hurt Timothy. I love him."

Mercy said, "I saw her put an evil-smelling green ointment on him! Every time she did it, he grew worse!"

Ann pointed at the rafters. "I see the ghost of my poor, dead baby sister! She's crying out for vengeance. Hannah's mother promised to heal baby Sarah, but she killed her! And she taught Hannah how to make her evil ointments!"

The room spun. How could Ann say this? They'd been friends. They'd sewn together, played together, grown up together.

"They're lying," Hannah shouted, her voice raspy. "Judge Hathorne, they're lying! How can you believe these fairytales?"

"Arrest Hannah True," Judge Hathorne instructed the guards.

"Please, Ann," Hannah begged. "Don't let them take me."

Why were they doing this? She'd told no one about Mercy's fortune-telling game; she'd kept her promise. Was it because she'd refused to join them? Because they'd dug themselves in too deep and couldn't risk getting caught?

"I'm innocent," Hannah cried. "I'm innocent!"

It was no use.

At the far end of the bench, Mercy's lips curled in a triumphant smile.

That smile felt like a stab to Hannah's heart.

FOURTEEN

O utside, the guards yanked Hannah roughly through
the crowd. She flinched as something hit her in the
head—a clod of horse dung. The cruel shouts were un-
bearable.

Isaac stood on the crowd's edge, but now he pushed
through. He wore his toolbelt and work clothes, as though
he'd come rushing from his father's forge. When he
reached Hannah's side, he shoved her in anger.

But then his hand was in hers, pressing something into
her fingers.

Startled, she closed her fist around it, slipping the hard
object into her skirt pocket.

The guards shoved her into the horse cart. It was a
struggle, for the prisoners were squeezed together like cat-
tle. Her family friends, the Proctors were there, along with
the scarf-pin-woman, Mistress English, and others who'd
supposedly feasted on blood out in the field.

The cart began moving.

When Hannah looked back, Isaac was gone.

"Where are they taking us?" Mistress English asked in a high, trembling voice.

"To the Boston jail," Goodman Proctor replied.

Elizabeth Proctor crawled over to sit beside Hannah and wrapped an arm around her. "Stay strong, child," she whispered. "We'll get this sorted out."

Hannah nodded.

But she knew there would be no sorting things out. Their only hope was to escape before they reached the jail —despite the guards on horseback flanking them on both sides.

Hannah had heard tales of the Boston jail; it was a place of murderers and thieves. Water often flooded the dungeon, and the foul-smelling muck rose to the prisoner's ankles.

"We have to get away," she whispered to her mother's friend.

"It's too dangerous, they'll kill us," Elizabeth Proctor murmured back.

"We're dead anyway," Hannah whispered. "We have to try."

The cart rumbled across a marshy area where insects attacked in droves. All the while, she hoped desperately for a chance to leap out and run away. But the guards never took their eyes from the prisoners.

The ride seemed to go on forever.

At midday, the caravan splashed across the Mystic River. What if she leaped into the rushing current? Maybe it would carry her to a distant bank, the waters moving too fast for them to catch her. She'd reach the shore, climb out, and disappear into the forest.

But she'd never survive. She couldn't swim.

The same thoughts crossed her mind at the Charles River.

Then the cart was loaded onto a boat and ferried across the water to Boston. The city loomed nearer and nearer.

It was over. She'd lost her chance.

The Boston wharf echoed with noise and clamor, unlike anything she'd ever seen. It was crammed with shipbuilders' yards, warehouses, and crowded taverns. Hannah's legs flexed with the urgent need to stand, to jump down, to run and run, and disappear down a shadowy lane.

"Now," she whispered to Goodwife Proctor.

"Hannah, no!"

But she was doing it. She rose, turning, placing her hands on the cart's frame. Eyeing the landing spot, tensing as she prepared to leap.

The guard acted swiftly. His hand connected with her head, hitting her hard. She fell back amidst the prisoners with her nose streaming blood.

"Try that again and you're dead," he roared. "All of you."

The other guards raised their clubs, making the prisoners cower.

Hannah choked back an outraged sob, swiping blood from her nose and chin. The cart rattled along narrow cobblestone streets with tall houses and fine shops. How could this be happening? She'd done nothing wrong. Nothing!

This was Mercy's doing. What had she ever done to Mercy to make her hate her so—apart from becoming friends with Ann?

The cart passed a burial ground with crooked gravestones.

Cold sweat coursed down Hannah's sides. How would it feel to hang to death? To put her head in the hangman's noose, to feel the eyes of her neighbors and friends on her, to have the stool yanked from beneath her feet?

That's what awaited her, unless she could escape.

The cart ground to a stop outside a foreboding stone building. From the jail's barred windows came awful screams and wails.

Inside it was so dark that one had to squint to see. The jail keeper, a Mr. Arnold, was a burly man with a wiry beard. He led them down a dirty corridor that reeked of damp and urine and shoved them into a cavernous dungeon with one small window.

Hannah recognized Tituba, Sarah Good, and others from their village in the gloom.

Mr. Arnold fixed a long chain with heavy iron shackles to Hannah's ankles.

Elizabeth Proctor cried out, "Why do we need these? She's only a child!"

"Each prisoner gets them," Mr. Arnold replied. "You also get bedding and food. The fee is two shillings, sixpence a week."

"What?" she cried out in disbelief. "We have to pay to be treated like this?"

"Your family will be responsible for your jail fees," Mr. Arnold said in a dull, monotone voice. "If the court rules you innocent, be warned. You will not be allowed to leave until you've paid all your fees."

John Proctor snorted.

Mr. Arnold didn't seem concerned. Instead, he yanked John Proctor back into the corridor. "You ain't staying with the ladies. Follow me."

Elizabeth Proctor cried out in anguish as they led her husband to the men's cells.

The group stood in stunned silence, and barely a moment passed before a new set of guards appeared.

"Mistress English?" one demanded.

The woman in her silk scarf hesitated before calling out in a resigned voice. "Here."

"Guess you're a rich lady, huh? You're to be taken to the good cells upstairs. Now move, let's go."

They had rich-people cells?

The leg irons bit into Hannah's ankles as the large wooden door was slammed shut and locked. She shuffled over to a corner where a few straw pallets lay. The stench from the overflowing latrine bucket against the far wall was overwhelming.

Hannah sank down with her back to the moldy wall. Rebecca Nurse, sitting nearby, nodded at her with sympathy. At the dungeon's far end, she spotted frail Sarah Osborne, who was huddled alongside the beggar-woman, Sarah Good.

A high-pitched keening startled her. With a shock, she saw Sarah Good's little daughter curled in a ball on the floor. They'd locked up a child? Would they hang her, too? Would anyone get out alive?

"Well, I never. Hannah True has joined the party," Sarah Good called out. "How do you come to be here, accused of being a witch? I thought those afflicted girls were your friends." She smirked.

Hannah's face felt hot with shame. "They are no friends of mine."

Sarah Good sniggered.

Rebecca Nurse said, "Leave her alone, we are all suffering and it's not her fault."

"Isn't it?" Sarah Good demanded.

A stranger spoke up. "I've never even been to Salem Village. I do not know how it is that I'm accused of being a witch by girls I've never met, from a place I've never been to."

"I'm so sorry," Hannah said.

"I don't blame you, child," the stranger said. "You're a victim, too. And a mere slip of a girl. It breaks my heart to see you in here."

Rebecca Nurse whispered in Hannah's ear. "Careful, my dear. That's Bridget Bishop. She owns a tavern and entertains men till the wee hours of the morn. They drink and gamble all night. Not the sort you want to befriend."

Hannah pulled away. "I don't care about gossip. She spoke kindly to me."

Rebecca Nurse donned a sour frown.

Somewhere, water dripped in a steady *plink, plink, plink*. The mildew-covered walls gave off a musty odor. Grit from the horse cart made Hannah's skin itch, and her parched throat ached.

Sickly Sarah Osborne began to cough—a loud, worrisome cough. "Oh please, Lord, let me die."

If only Hannah had herbs and a kettle, she could make Sarah Osborne feel better. "You need a warm drink."

"There's none you'll find in here."

"Take my cloak," Hannah said, hobbling over to Goody Osborne.

"No! You'll catch a chill."

"Just for a little while, I'll come for it later." Before the woman could refuse, Hannah straightened. As she did, something hard jabbed her side.

It was the item from Isaac; she'd been too afraid to pull it out during their journey. Maybe it held hope, although hope seemed unlikely.

Wanting to study it in private, she made her way to the latrine bucket. Gagging at the stench, she waited for the women to turn away.

What had Isaac given her? He'd risked his own safety, running at her like that. When he'd stood before her, the whole world had seemed to stop. She'd never forget his agonized eyes—he'd spoken a million things and yet he'd said nothing at all.

Carefully, she pulled out the object.

It was a metal file!

Her fingers tightened around it. Isaac must have had it in his toolbelt. He must have thought she could file through the jail cell window. It was exactly the kind of quick thinking she'd expect from him.

"Thank you," she whispered.

It was a beautiful gift, and she'd treasure it until her last breath.

But Isaac could never have guessed she'd be locked in a dungeon with only one small opening. He'd never know the window was entirely out of reach.

Hannah held it for a long moment, running her thumb along the rough surface and deciding it was the most beautiful thing in the world.

Then she tucked it away and shuffled back to her spot.

Dark despair washed over her, deeper than the dungeon that held her prisoner. She'd never see Isaac to thank him. She'd never be able to tell him what a good friend he was.

She'd never be free again.

FIFTEEN

That night, rats scurried in the blackness while women snored and water dripped. The smell of earth, mildew, unwashed bodies, and the latrine bucket stung her nostrils.

At dawn, the door opened and the bulky figure of Mr. Arnold put a tray laden with bowls on the floor. The food was a grey, tasteless porridge but Hannah gulped it down.

"I can't eat it," Bridget Bishop told Hannah. "It's like glue. How did you manage it?"

"Plug your nose and swallow," Hannah said.

Bridget Bishop giggled, and Hannah couldn't help smiling back.

Plugging her nose, Bridget Bishop tipped down a mouthful, then made a funny, gruesome face. "I bet Mistress English in her fancy cell doesn't have to eat this slop."

It felt good to laugh in the midst of their terror.

Later that morning, Mr. Arnold returned. "Form a line. We're going out to the prison yard."

"Thank the Lord," Rebecca Nurse said.

Outside, Hannah squinted in the dazzling sun. High wooden fences surrounded the rectangular dirt yard. Beyond the fences, gulls cried.

A few benches bordered one wall. Mistress English sat there alone, still dressed in her now grimy silk scarf and fancy clothes. She smiled as Hannah approached.

"It's Hannah, isn't it?" she asked.

"Yes. Good morrow, Mistress English."

"I remember you from the trial. I wanted to thank you. It was a very brave thing you did. You put yourself in jeopardy because you would not accuse me of sticking you with my pin."

"I should have said more. I should have spoken up earlier."

"Truly, would that have helped? I think not. Those girls accused you. I'm so sorry that you're here, my dear." She patted the bench beside her. When Hannah sat, Mistress English spoke in a low voice. "Don't worry. Even now my husband, Mr. English, is planning to help me escape. I will do everything in my power to help you, too."

Before Hannah could ask how, a commotion arose on the far side of the prison yard.

"Guards!" someone shouted. "This woman . . . she's fainted!"

Hannah leaped to her feet. It was frail Sarah Osborne. The woman lay on the ground, her face ashen. Hannah ran and knelt beside her, heart racing, trying to think what her mother would do. She listened for breath but could hear nothing.

"Get up, woman!" a guard barked, nudging Sarah Osborne with his boot.

"A bucket of cold water will help," another laughed.

"Stop!" Hannah shouted, fighting off tears. "I think she's dead."

"Stand aside." A guard raised his club at Hannah. "Now!"

"She was kind," Hannah cried. "She didn't deserve this!"

"I said stand aside!" The guard's club came down, but Mistress English yanked Hannah clear.

Sweet old Sarah Osborne should never have been in this filthy prison. Now she was dead. Did Hannah's friends have any idea what they'd done?

Mercy had worn a look of triumph when they'd dragged Hannah away. She'd known she was sentencing Hannah to death.

Hannah wouldn't let Mercy win.

She refused to go down without a fight.

She would get out of there, no matter what.

"Hannah True?" Mr. Arnold called, opening the cell door the following morning.

Hannah steeled herself as the prison keeper unlocked her shackles and led her down a long, cell-lined corridor.

Was this it, then? Was she being called to trial?

"I've been informed that you were trained as a village healer," Mr. Arnold said.

Hannah glanced up, startled.

"You attempted to help the prisoner who died yesterday," he said.

Was he going to accuse her of causing Sarah Osborne's death?

"Yes . . . she was sickly and—"

Mr. Arnold interrupted. "The prisoner, Mistress English, requires your medical advice. You have five minutes to talk with her." He unlocked one of the cells.

Mistress English sat on a narrow bed. It was a simple room with a stone floor and a barred window that looked out over an alley, yet it seemed luxurious compared to the dark dungeon.

He locked Hannah inside and strode away.

"Sit, quickly," Mistress English said.

Hannah sat beside her, concerned. "Have you fallen ill?"

"No, listen, I'm trying to get you into a cell next to my own. I've told Mr. Arnold that I need your help. I will pay for the cell if he allows it."

The idea of leaving behind the smelly dungeon filled her with hope.

Mistress English said, "My husband and I have influential friends who believe in our innocence. We own a ship, *The Grace*. They'll help sneak us aboard, and we'll sail for New York, where we'll be safe. Hannah, I want you on that ship tomorrow."

Heart thumping, she said, "Tomorrow? But how?"

"Mr. Arnold allows me to leave the jail for a few hours a day, as long as I'm accompanied by a guard," she replied. "Fortunately, my guard is a greedy fellow, and my husband has paid him off. But we must think of a way to get you to the ship, too."

"If only my dungeon window wasn't so high!" Hannah touched the spot where she'd hidden Isaac's file, tucked into the waistband of her undergarments.

The door burst open.

Mistress English took a raspy breath and fanned herself weakly.

"What ails Mistress English?" Mr. Arnold asked Hannah.

Mistress English said, "It is good of you to care for my welfare. Thank you, Mr. Arnold, for allowing her to see me."

"Madam, this is not about your welfare. I am a warden. You may be wealthy and you may have purchased special favors, but you are still a witch. I will not have you die before justice is done. I want you kept alive long enough to stand trial and meet the punishment you deserve."

"Of course," Mistress English said.

In a steady voice, Hannah said, "I'm afraid she has the vapors—a condition that will require me to watch over her night and day." To make it more convincing, she added, "I need healing herbs, if you want her to live."

"Herbs?" Mr. Arnold crossed his arms. "You won't be making witches' potions in my prison!"

"I'm only asking for simple herbs like thyme and rosemary. The same your wife probably uses for cooking."

He scowled. "My wife is no witch!"

"Of course not."

Mistress English gasped for breath, "Oh my heart, it's beating so fast."

"Please, Mr. Arnold," Hannah said. "I must fix her a tea as soon as possible."

"I'll be back." Mr. Arnold locked the door behind him.

Hannah carefully removed the file and showed it to Mistress English. "I could probably saw through the window bars with this."

Her eyes lit in surprise. "Well done, yes, you could."

They had no more time to discuss the plan. Mr. Arnold reappeared and Hannah had to quickly hide the file under her skirts.

"The herbs will be brought to the dungeon," he said. "Along with a kettle of boiled water. You will prepare the tea down there and I will carry it up to Mistress English. Come, it's time to go."

"I'd prefer her to stay here with me," Mistress English

said. "Or at least in a cell nearby. You heard her. She needs to watch over me day and night. I'm ill!"

But Mr. Arnold snorted, "These jail cells are not for the likes of her. They're for a better class of prisoner."

"I can pay."

Mr. Arnold shook his head. "This wench belongs in the dungeons."

Mistress English and Hannah exchanged an alarmed glance.

They'd failed.

Hannah's heart sank as Mr. Arnold led her back down the grimy corridors, shoved her into the dungeon, and slammed the heavy door.

SIXTEEN

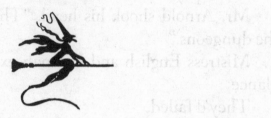

The next morning, Mr. Arnold entered the dungeon wearing a snide grin.

"Breakfast," he said. "Eat quickly. Could be your last meal! Some of you are being transported to Salem Town for your final trial. Then, I suppose you'll be found guilty and hanged."

"Who is going?" Hannah demanded.

"Let's see, well, Rebecca Nurse, for one," he said.

The Putnam's neighbor, who'd argued with them over land ownership and now found herself in jail, let out a frightened cry.

"But she's innocent!" Hannah said.

"That's for the jurors to decide. Time to go."

Guards tied Rebecca Nurse's hands. Next came Bridget Bishop, the woman who'd laughed with Hannah over the awful food. Last came the beggar-woman, Sarah Good.

"But what about my little girl?" she cried.

The child clung to her mother's skirts for dear life.

"The little witch can stay in the dungeon," Mr. Arnold said.

"She needs her mother!" Hannah said.

Elizabeth Proctor whispered, "Hannah, hush. Don't draw attention to yourself."

Hannah's stomach churned with horror and fury.

A guard tore the child from her mother's skirts and shoved her to the ground. She ran for the door, reaching it as it slammed shut. She hammered it with her tiny fists screaming, "Mommy!"

Tituba crept forward and wrapped her arms around the girl. The child allowed herself to be picked up and wept into Tituba's shoulder.

"Will they be hanged?" Hannah asked Elizabeth Proctor.

"It's in God's hands now," she said quietly. "That poor child. But she's not the only child I fear for . . . I'm pregnant."

Hannah gasped. "You're pregnant?"

"My poor baby." She touched her belly and swallowed visibly. "What will become of her?"

Hannah drew in a breath. "Don't you see? That's good news! They won't hang you, not if you're pregnant. They wouldn't dare."

After a beat, she nodded. "You may be right. Hannah. I wish I could save you from this place. Your mother must be looking down in agony."

"I haven't given up yet," Hannah said.

They fell silent and Elizabeth Proctor began to pray.

But Hannah had no intention of placing her future in prayers alone. Again she eyed the high, narrow window. If only she could reach it, she might be able to escape.

Time was running out. It was already late morning. With a sinking feeling, she realized the kindly Mistress English was probably on board her ship, sailing away to New York.

At least one of them was free.

The following day, when Hannah shuffled out to the prison yard for exercise, she blinked with astonishment.

Mistress English sat on her usual bench. Dark circles shone blue under her eyes.

Hannah hurried over.

Mistress English took her arm and urged her to sit. When the guards turned away, she whispered, "I have bad news from Salem."

"Tell me."

"Bridget Bishop was found guilty." She paused, her grip tightening. "They escorted her to the hill outside the village. They hung her from a tree until she was dead."

Hannah let out an involuntary sob.

"The whole village watched," Mistress English said.

Had Mercy, Ann, Abigail, and Lizzie been there? It was unthinkable. Did they finally realize what they'd done? Bridget Bishop had been kind and funny. And most important, she'd been *innocent!*

Would her *friends* watch Hannah hang, too? Would none of them defend her?

Hannah's fingers went to her throat. She turned to Mistress English. "Why haven't you escaped?"

"We ran into a problem. But tomorrow, we'll try again. Child, I have to get you into a cell near mine. I'll offer Mr. Arnold more money."

"He's already said no."

The guards walked past and they both stopped talking.

Finally, Mistress English said, "Every man has his price, you'll see. Tonight, you'll have to saw through the window bars. Tomorrow morning, I'll wait for you in the alleyway outside your new cell."

Hannah nodded, but she knew it would never work. Mr. Arnold was not a man who could be bribed.

Suddenly, a crazy idea began to form.

"I know what to do—" she began.

"Break time's over!" a guard shouted. "Everyone back inside."

SEVENTEEN

A few hours later, afternoon shadows stretched across the dungeon's mucky floor. Soon, it would be night.

Hannah's knees crumpled under her and she fell to the ground.

"Hannah!" Elizabeth Proctor cried out, crouching next to her. "What's wrong?"

"I'm sooo hot," Hannah moaned. "My head's burning."

"But this room is freezing!" Elizabeth replied.

"I don't feel well." Hannah clutched her stomach.

Mr. Arnold was called. He arrived in a hurry. The women turned to him with urgent cries.

Hidden behind their skirts, Hannah stuck her fingers down her throat, gagged, and vomited on the floor.

"What is this?" Mr. Arnold demanded. "What's wrong with you?"

90

"My head hurts, and I have a strange rash under my clothes."

Mr. Arnold's eyes widened. The prisoners edged away.

"I don't want to die!" Hannah cried. "Oh the pain, oh my head, oh my stomach!" She bent double. "Why is it so hot?"

"This child is very sick," Elizabeth Proctor said. Still, even she had stepped back, one protective hand covering her pregnant belly. "She needs a doctor."

"I'm so scared," Hannah whimpered. "What if it's the pox?"

"The pox?" Mr. Arnold roared in a voice edged with terror.

"We're all going to catch it!" Tituba took Sarah Good's

little girl by the hand and hauled her to the dungeon's farthest side.

Others followed.

"You must get away from me," Hannah warned her mother's friend.

Mr. Arnold, however, threw a set of keys at Elizabeth Proctor. "Unlock her."

With trembling fingers, she unlocked the shackles. "Don't worry, child," she said, trying to comfort Hannah. "You're young and strong. Surely you will recover."

"Get up," Mr. Arnold ordered. "You'll not be allowed to infect my prisoners."

Hannah stumbled to her feet.

Keeping a good distance, he led her to a half-empty corridor of cells. "Inside," he barked, opening a cell door.

Hannah obeyed, clutching her belly and coughing.

Mr. Arnold slammed the door shut and practically ran off.

When she was sure he'd gone, she straightened and looked around. He'd stuck her in a cell with a window, not far from Mistress English's cell—and she could see the alley outside!

It had worked. Her plan had actually worked.

It was her first small triumph.

Hannah was desperate to start filing at the bars.

Finally, darkness fell and she set to work.

To her dismay, the bars were so much tougher than she'd imagined. Thick, rough iron, wider than her thumb. Was it even possible to saw through? The noise was awful, making her cringe. Back and forth, back and forth the rhythmic scraping echoed. Heart racing, she constantly looked over one shoulder.

No guards yet. How long would her luck hold?

After what felt like forever, her heart sank. It was hopeless! She'd only managed to chip away at a small part. The night was more than half gone. Tears of frustration rolled down her cheeks. Her arms, shoulders, and wrists ached, and her head nodded from exhaustion.

She kept going.

When dawn's grey light colored the alleyway outside, she panicked.

She'd never break out in time. Mr. Arnold would discover the damage and know she'd tried to get away.

She had to get out!

Desperate, she hauled at one bar. *Come on, come on!*

She gasped as it shifted a little, and a bit of stone near the base crumbled.

One more tug, and it came completely loose from the wall!

Her success gave her new energy. She threw it on the ground and began sawing frantically on a second bar.

Footsteps sounded outside the jail. Someone was in the alleyway, and they were approaching the window. It had to be a guard patrolling the exterior. Not now, she'd almost broken through!

Heart in her throat, she shrank against the wall.

A whisper. "Hannah!"

She peered outside to see a dark silhouette in a bonnet.

"Mistress English?" she cried.

"Shhh! Yes, hurry, climb out. Mr. English is keeping a

lookout at the end of the alley. But there are guards everywhere."

"I only cut one bar. I need more time!"

"Oh dear! Mr. Arnold will be bringing your breakfast —he'll be at your cell any minute. You must wait. Once he's gone, you can keep working . . ."

But they both knew Hannah had lost her chance at freedom. She'd never be able to escape in broad daylight.

Mistress English hesitated, despair in her eyes. Then she removed her cloak and pushed it through the window. "Here, it has a hood to disguise you."

The rattle of the jailer's keys echoed inside the jail's hallway. Horrible Mr. Arnold was coming.

"Go," Hannah whispered urgently, "Don't worry about me. I'll find my way. I'll meet you at the ship."

Mistress English fled.

Hannah turned as the door creaked open, hiding the file under her skirts.

Mr. Arnold stood there with a scarf covering his mouth and nose.

With her back shadowing the damaged window, she swallowed hard.

He set down a bowl of porridge and nudged it into the cell. "The doctor will be here to see you later today."

Hannah said nothing, willing him to go. The bar she'd torn free lay to one side. She should have kicked it out of view!

His eyes wandered across her face.

Then, as if reading her mind, his gaze drifted toward the ground.

EIGHTEEN

Hannah rushed toward her jailer and coughed hard in his face.

"Nasty little witch," Mr. Arnold snarled, clearly frightened, and slammed the heavy cell door.

She whirled and set to work on the second bar. Faster now, she filed at a speed she'd never have thought herself capable. The file burned hot as fire in her fingers. Sweat dripped into her eyes. The tang of shaved metal filled her nostrils.

And the bar was starting to feel wobbly.

She pulled.

Nothing.

She pulled again, grinding her teeth and propping one foot against the wall.

All of a sudden, the bar popped free. She flew backward and landed on her dish of porridge, sending it splatting everywhere as the dust settled.

Rushing to the window, she found she could just fit her head through.

It wasn't large enough.

Any moment, a guard could glance into the alley and discover her with her head poking out.

She started sawing again but the third bar wouldn't

give. Maybe if she got her shoulders outside, maybe if she wiggled really hard—

Voices sounded from within the jail. Someone was coming.

It was now or never. She had to try. She squeezed her head out the gap, then her shoulders, then her ribs. She could barely breathe as she pulled and shoved, her hands bleeding, her clothes tearing.

Her hips were through.

For a brief moment, she hung suspended by her knees, dangling in the grimy alley. She fell the rest of the way, smashing onto the cobblestones below.

Searing pain flashed through her skull. She lay making a horrible rasping noise. But she had to move.

Head throbbing, shoulders aching, bloody hands on fire, she scurried through the shadows to the lane's far end. Only then did she risk a glance back at her cell.

No one was there.

Her escape hadn't been discovered. Yet.

Creeping to the alley's edge, she peered around the corner. Guards patrolled the prison's front entrance. She froze in dread—how would she ever get away without being seen?

Just then, the jail's front door opened.

Mr. Arnold appeared carrying a big tray with what appeared to be the guards' breakfast. The guards approached him, their attention on the food.

It was time.

She took a deep breath, stepped out onto the main road, and started walking briskly in the opposite direction of the jail.

Every bone in her body wanted to run, but she forced herself to walk like she was just a regular citizen out for a morning stroll. Was she even headed in the right direction? Where was the harbor, the boat? She had no clue. All she could think was that the guards would suddenly notice her and shout the alarm.

As soon as she reached a narrow side street, she turned. She could hear her heartbeat thumping in her ears.

With no idea of how to find the ship, she kept going, praying that a girl wandering alone at dawn wouldn't draw attention.

Ahead, a woman emptied a bucket of smelly water into the street without looking up. On a front stoop, a black cat stretched its legs and yawned. A wagon rattled past, forcing her to press against a wall.

She hurried down a crooked lane where tall, narrow houses cast deep shadows. To her alarm, the lane looped around, returning her to within a block of the jail where she'd begun.

Panic rose. She'd been walking in circles!

She quickened her pace and reached an intersection. Here was something she recognized—a sign with a bright green dragon that read *The Green Dragon Tavern*. The prison cart had passed by here when she'd arrived in Boston, after they'd disembarked from the ferry. The tavern had been close to the wharf. That could mean only one thing: the waterfront had to be nearby.

The soft shuffle of footprints startled her. Someone grabbed her arm.

"Well, well, well, who is this?" asked a gruff voice.

Hannah froze, fear flooding her veins. "I'm no one. Let me go."

"Are you lost?" The man had a red face and a scruffy beard. His eyes glittered.

"No," she lied.

"Why don't you come inside the tavern and have some beer?" He winked and his breath reeked of alcohol.

In a loud, clear voice, she said. "My Papa will be looking for me, and he won't like you touching my arm! So let go, right now."

He jumped away as if he'd been burned. "Your Papa, hey? I don't see him."

"He's coming up from the docks this very minute. He's a sailor, and a big one."

The scruffy man said, "Well, you're going the wrong way if you're headed toward the wharf. It's down there." He pointed ahead.

"I know that," she said.

"Do you now?" His eyes twinkled. "So then, you must know you make a turn at *The Heart and Crown*, then take *Red Lyon Lane*. You'll pass the *British Coffee House*. Then, you'll see all the ships ahead of you."

Hannah stared at him, surprised.

He doubled over, laughing. "You're not much of a liar, lassie. So aren't you going to reward me with a kiss?"

"No, but thank you." She pulled her cloak tighter and ran.

How long would Mistress English keep the ship waiting? They might have already set sail. Ahead, the *British Coffee House* came into view. Boys in work clothes trudged along, yawning in the early light. The ocean's unmistakable tang filled the air. She still had to find where *The Grace* was docked, and she had to do it fast.

Had the jailer discovered her empty cell? Had he sent out the guards? Were they combing Boston's streets for her right now?

She reached the wharf, breathing hard.

Great wooden warehouses bustled with rough-looking men who unloaded barrels that smelled of molasses, drying fish, and spices.

Further down, a sight made her heart leap into her throat: ships.

Almost there.

Sprinting, she arrived at the prow of the first. To her disappointment, the boat that smelled of strong spices had the name *Rajah* painted on the hull. Next, she arrived at a fine schooner named *Deliverance*.

But where was *The Grace*? What if they'd left without her? What would she do? .

She squinted into the sun, trying to read the name of the next ship in line. Up on its pointed prow, a woman stood silhouetted against the rising sun. The woman held one hand at her brow as though searching for someone.

A great lump formed in Hannah's throat. They'd waited.

"Mistress English!" Hannah shouted.

The woman didn't hear.

"Mistress English!" she yelled at the top of her lungs and threw back her hood.

Men turned to stare, taking in her face that was dirty from being locked in a filthy prison cell, her matted hair, and her bloody hands that now oozed from where she'd hurt herself on the cell's iron bars.

Of all the bad luck, a fancy carriage came rattling along, and in the back was none other than Judge Hathorne. *The judge from the trial!* Had he recognized her? One thing was certain; he was headed her way.

On deck, Mistress English had disappeared.

She heard the creak of the gangplank being lowered. Birds wheeled and screeched overhead. Hannah whispered a prayer. A man appeared on *The Grace*, just where Mistress English had stood.

Throwing all caution to the wind, Hannah made up her mind. In a high, girlish voice, completely unlike her own, she called out to him. "Father, I'm down here, I got lost trying to find my way back."

"Charlotte, there you are," he called. "You gave us a fright. Hurry on board, your mother is looking everywhere for you."

Judge Hathorne spoke to the carriage driver and the

carriage slowed. She felt the man's stern gaze studying her face. She lowered her head and hurried past.

The gangplank was mere feet away.

She waited for the shout. It didn't come. The wooden walkway shook under her tired feet. The ship bobbed and the ropes creaked. Hannah turned back.

The carriage had come to a full stop

Judge Hathorne squinted at her for a long moment. Then he shook his head, as if he'd mixed her up with someone else. With a word to the driver, the horses set off.

Hannah reached the entrance.

Mistress English stood waiting in the shadows, her face ashen. "Hannah! Thank God you're safe!"

Hannah stumbled toward her and fell into her open arms. Mistress English held her tight and, for a moment, Hannah could almost imagine it was her mother holding her close.

She realized that the Englishes had been waiting for her, even though every minute had put them in more danger of being caught.

Just then, the man from the deck appeared. "That was clever thinking," he said. Although his rugged face was lined with anxiety, he grinned.

"You were clever, too," Hannah said, grinning back.

"I'm Mr. English, but I think you guessed that already. My wife has told me all about you, but there will be time for talk later. We must set sail before we fugitives are caught!"

"Thank you. Thank you so much," Hannah said.

Mr. English instructed the sailors to raise the gangplank and cast off.

The three of them stood together at the railing and watched silently as Boston receded into the distance. Hannah thought of her old home and of Isaac. He had been her one true friend. She wished she could tell him that his file had saved her life.

"Will we ever come back?" she asked.

"A terrible madness has taken place here. But perhaps one day . . ." The wind tossed the hair against Mistress English's cheeks.

Hannah shivered. It *had* seemed like a terrible madness. Had any of it been real? There were so many others that hadn't been as lucky as she was. She closed her eyes, praying for those who had been left behind, for those who had been unjustly accused, praying they'd find their way to freedom.

As the land disappeared, she inhaled the fresh air blowing off the ocean and relief flooded through her. Mistress English's hand found hers and they held on tight.

Hannah was finally safe.

Somehow she'd done it. She'd escaped the Salem witch trials.

10 FAST FACTS ABOUT
THE SALEM WITCH TRIALS

1. The trials took place from 1692-1693.
2. The location was a village near Boston, Massachusetts.
3. A group of girls fell ill: they screamed, made weird noises and had strange fits.
4. The girls claimed that witches sent their spirits to attack them.
5. Adults took the girls seriously: they arrested the "witches" and put them on trial.
6. Accusations began to spread: people turned on one another, and hysteria took hold.
7. By the end, over 200 people had been accused.
8. 19 people were hung, one man was pressed to death, and others died in prison awaiting judgment.
9. Some say the trials were motivated by political and religious disagreements.
10. In 2001, over 300 years later, then Governor of Massachusetts, Jane Swift, finally proclaimed the victims innocent.

DOWNLOAD THIS BOOK'S STUDY GUIDE AT:
scottpetersbooks.com/worksheets

DID YOU KNOW?

WHAT WERE THE SALEM WITCH TRIALS?

During the winter of 1692, several girls suffered strange fits—they screamed and made strange sounds, threw things, crawled under furniture, and contorted their bodies into weird positions. The girls complained that witches had sent their spirits to attack them by pinching them and jabbing them with pins. They accused neighbors in their village of practicing witchcraft.

At the same time, townspeople were arguing over land rights and religious differences.

As the situation escalated, neighboring towns started accusing people of witchcraft, too. The guilty were put on trial and sentenced.

WHERE WAS SALEM VILLAGE?

Salem Village and Salem Town were located on America's east coast, in the state of Massachusetts, about an hour's drive north of Boston. After the trials, Salem Village changed its name to Danvers because residents hoped to forget the horrible event that happened there.

HOW MANY PEOPLE WERE ACCUSED?

Over two hundred were accused. Most were women, but men were accused, too.

WHAT HAPPENED TO THE ACCUSED?

Of the two hundred accused, thirty were found guilty. Fourteen women and five men were hung. One man was pressed to death with heavy rocks because he would not confess. Others died in prison while awaiting trial. After the governor's own wife was accused of witchcraft, the trials finally ended.

WHAT CAUSED THE SALEM WITCH TRIALS?

Even to this day, no one is sure what caused this tragedy. Was it hysteria or a need for attention? Was it based on arguments over land rights and religious differences? Could the girls have fallen ill due to some environmental poisoning, such as fungus on the rye crops? Perhaps we will never know. Maybe the biggest mystery is why community leaders believed the girls and sentenced so many innocent people to death.

THE AFFLICTED

Historically, there were numerous afflicted—too many

to include in one story. According to records, here's the part our characters played.

ELIZABETH PARRIS: Nine-year-old "Betty" was sent to live with relatives in Salem Town during the trials to protect her from witches. She did not testify at the trials.

ABIGAIL WILLIAMS: Eleven-year-old Abigail accused fifty-seven people of witchcraft. Rumors suggest she fled the village when the trials ended.

ANN PUTNAM: Twelve-year-old Ann Putnam accused sixty-two people of witchcraft. She was the only afflicted girl to apologize for her role in the trials.

Below is part of her confession:

. . . I can truly and uprightly say, before God and man, I did it not out of any anger, malice, or ill-will to any person, for I had no such thing against one of them; but what I did was ignorantly, being deluded by Satan. And particularly, as I was a chief instrument of accusing of Goodwife Nurse and her two sisters, I desire to lie in the dust, and to be humbled for it, in that I was a cause, with others, of so sad a calamity to them and their families; for which cause I desire to lie in the dust, and earnestly beg forgiveness of God, and from all those unto whom I have given just cause of sorrow and offense, whose relations were taken away or accused . . .

MERCY LEWIS: Seventeen-year-old Mercy testified against Reverend Burroughs, who was hanged. She accused eight others and testified in sixteen cases.

ELIZABETH HUBBARD: Seventeen-year-old Lizzie testified against twenty-nine people. Some people tried to discredit her testimony, calling her a compulsive liar with an extremely vivid imagination.

JOHN INDIAN: Tituba's husband might have pretended to be afflicted to avoid being accused like his wife. What happened to him after the trial is unknown.

THE ACCUSED

Over two hundred people were accused. According to records, here's what happened to those in our story.

TITUBA, the Parris's slave was from Barbados. She was one of the few who confessed to witchcraft and escaped the hangman's noose. However, she was stuck in jail for a year because Reverend Parris refused to pay her jail fees.

SARAH GOOD, the village beggar, refused to confess to witchcraft. She had a baby in jail and was later hanged.

DORCAS GOOD, the four-year-old daughter of Sarah, remained in jail until December 1692, when her father could finally afford to pay her jail fees.

SARAH OSBORNE, the frail older woman, was ill when the girls accused her of witchcraft. The damp jail worsened her illness and she died in prison.

BRIDGET BISHOP had previously been in trouble with the law: she fought with her husband in public and had been accused of witchcraft in the past. She was the first to be hanged.

REBECCA NURSE had a strong defense. Her family and thirty-nine neighbors signed a petition to clear her name. It worked, she was found not guilty. However, in an awful turn of events, her accusers protested, the court changed its mind, and she was hanged.

ELIZABETH PROCTOR was pregnant in prison and avoided being hanged. She gave birth in jail and was later released.

MARY ENGLISH, (Mistress English) escaped by boat to New York. She and her husband waited until the hysteria ended, and returned to Salem the following summer. To their dismay, their property had been seized: their house, fourteen buildings, twenty-one ships, a wharf, and a ware-house. They never got their property back.

MEMORIALS

In 1992, on the Salem Trials 300th anniversary, a memorial park was constructed. It contains a number of stone benches, one dedicated to each of the victims.

In addition, a stone monument was erected with an inscription that reads:

In memory of those innocents who died during the Salem Village witchcraft hysteria of 1692.

Every year, people curious about this terrible yet fascinating part of American history flock to Salem, which can still be visited today. To learn more, visit: www.salem.org

Ten Fascinating Facts about the Puritans

1. The Puritans arrived in Massachusetts in 1630 aboard seventeen ships.
2. They set up a religious community, which was known for its strict, unforgiving beliefs.
3. They often named their children after Bible characters—that's why we have so many Sarahs in this story. They also named them after valued traits, such as Comfort, Constance, Prudence, and Fear. Some names were really bizarre—Make Peace, Be Faithful, Fight the Good Fight of Faith, and Kill Sin!
4. Puritan dyed their clothing a variety of colors using vegetable dyes. The upperclass favored bright, deep colors like purple and red. Clothes were simple, and there was a law against "wearing excessive lace".
5. Puritans were intolerant of other religious groups, even though they came to America to practice religious freedom.
6. The Puritans believed in the devil, and that

devil-worshipping witches could curse them with bad luck.

7. Puritans did not celebrate Christmas. They thought it was a pagan custom with no biblical basis.

8. Puritans linked certain diseases to sin. For example, someone with a toothache may have sinned with his teeth by overeating—or by saying evil things. They believed prayer was the best cure. However, they also employed bloodletting (bleeding patients by making small cuts), tying fish to a patient's feet, and administrating a broth of boiled toad!

9. The Puritans rarely bathed. Most thought water was unhealthy and that dirt protected them from illness.

10. Most people had only two or three outfits and keeping them clean was hard. Laundry piled up in winter because the water would freeze.

DOWNLOAD THIS BOOK'S STUDY GUIDE AT:
scottpetersbooks.com/worksheets

THE I ESCAPED SERIES

I Escaped North Korea!

I Escaped The California Camp Fire

I Escaped The World's Deadliest Shark Attack

I Escaped Amazon River Pirates

I Escaped The Donner Party

I Escaped The Salem Witch Trials

Coming Soon:

I Escaped Pirates in the Caribbean

MORE BOOKS BY SCOTT PETERS

Mystery of the Egyptian Scroll

Mystery of the Egyptian Mummy

JOIN THE I ESCAPED CLUB

We're always coming out with new adventures,

so be sure to sign up for updates and news at:

https://www.subscribepage.com/escapedclub

Bibliography

Coughlin, Michelle Marchetti. *One Colonial Woman's World: The Life and Writings of Mehetabel Chandler Coit.* Boston: University of Massachusetts Press, 2012

Fraustino, Lisa Rowe. *I Walk in Dread: the Diary of Deliverance Trembley, Witness to the Salem Witch Trials.* Dear America Series. New York: Scholastic, 2004

Raum, Elizabeth. *The Dreadful, Smelly Colonies: The Disgusting details about Life in Colonial America.* Minnesota: Capstone Press, 2010

Rinaldi, Ann. *A Break with Charity : a Story about the Salem Witch Trials.* Orlando: Harcourt, 2003

Roach, Marilynne K. *The Salem Witch Trials: A Day-by-Day Chronicle of a Community Under Siege.* Maryland: Taylor Trade Pub, 2004

Roach, Marilynne K. *Six Women of Salem: the Untold Story of the Accused and Their Accusers in the Salem Witch Trials.* Boston: Da Capo Press, 2013

Schanzer, Rosalyn. *Witches! The Absolutely True Tale of Disaster in Salem.* Washington D.C.: National Geographic Society, 2011

Speare, Elizabeth George, *The Witch of Blackbird Pond.* Boston: Houghton Mifflin, 1958

Yolen, Jane. *The Salem Witch Trials: An Unsolved Mystery from History.* New York: Simon and Schuster Books for Young Readers, 2004